The Big Book of
Funny Stories

Jeremy Strong

The Big Book of Funny Stories

Illustrated by Nick Sharratt

Published by the Penguin Group
Penguin Books Ltd, 27 Wrights Lane, London W8 5TZ, England
Penguin Putnam Inc., 375 Hudson Street, New York, New York 10014, USA
Penguin Books Australia Ltd, Ringwood, Victoria, Australia
Penguin Books Canada Ltd, 10 Alcorn Avenue, Toronto, Ontario, Canada M4V 3B2
Penguin Books (NZ) Ltd, Private Bag 102902, NSMC, Auckland, New Zealand

On the World Wide Web at: *www.penguin.com*

Penguin Books Ltd, Registered Offices: Harmondsworth, Middlesex, England

The Indoor Pirates first published by Dutton 1995; published in Puffin Books 1997
The Indoor Pirates on Treasure Island first published in Puffin Books 1998
Giant Jim and the Hurricane first published by Viking 1997; published in Puffin Books 1999

This edition published by Viking 2000
3 5 7 9 10 8 6 4 2

Text copyright © Jeremy Strong, 1995, 1997, 1998
Illustrations copyright © Nick Sharratt, 1995, 1997, 1998
All rights reserved

The moral right of the author and illustrator has been asserted

Printed and bound in Great Britain by The Bath Press, Bath

British Library Cataloguing in Publication Data
A CIP catalogue record for this book is available from the British Library

ISBN 0–670–89359–5

Contents

Jeremy Strong

The
Indoor Pirates

Illustrated by Nick Sharratt

Contents

Introducing the Indoor Pirates

Blackpatch came from a
long line of pirates, and he
really did have a patch too
– although it was not
over one eye. It was on
the sleeve of his jacket,
where he had torn it on a
nail. His grandparents had
been pirates. His mother and
father had been pirates. It
seemed obvious that he should be a pirate
too. This was just a little unfortunate,
because Blackpatch hated the sea. In fact,
he hated water of any kind – drinking-water,
bath-water, washing-up water – and most
of all sea-water. Blackpatch wished he
didn't have to go on boats at all.

One day he got a letter from his great-grandmother, who was very ancient. She was 107, and she had patches too. There was one on her dress, one on her leather smoking-jacket (she *loved* big cigars), and another on her thumb, where she had cut it by mistake. It was quite a nasty cut, and it made Great-granny realize that she was getting too old to look after herself properly. She wanted her great-grandson to come home and see to her needs. The letter made Blackpatch very happy. At last he could live on dry land!

Off he went, and he looked after Great-granny very well until she died. (By this time she was 112.) Great-granny left her house to Blackpatch, saying that she hoped he would look after it, and the first thing that Blackpatch did was to write a letter of his own. He wrote to all his friends at sea – all the ones who didn't like it, and he asked them to come and live with him at 25 Dolphin Street. And that was how the Indoor Pirates began.

First of all, there was Bald Ben. He had huge muscles and was immensely strong. He could lift up two people at once, one under each arm. He hadn't a single hair on his bald head. Instead, right in the middle, he had a colourful tattoo of a rose, with I LOVE MUM written underneath. Bald Ben didn't like going to sea because it meant missing too much television.

Polly and Molly were twin sisters. They looked just like each other, except that Polly's hair was bunched out by her right

ear, and Molly's was bunched by her left
ear. They were always, ALWAYS arguing
with each other. Whatever one said, the
other said the opposite, even if it was
nonsense.

'We're sisters,' Polly might say.

'No, we're not!' Molly would snap.
'We're . . .' and she would screw up her
eyes desperately '. . . brothers!'

'You're stupid,' Polly would answer.

'You're the one that's stupid,' Molly
would counter, and so it would go on. The

twins didn't like going to sea because they couldn't swim.

The fifth and last Indoor Pirate was Lumpy Lawson. He didn't look lumpy at all – in fact, he was tall and rather skinny with it, despite his love of food. No matter how much he ate, he never got any fatter. Lumpy Lawson did all the cooking (and most of the shopping too) and whenever he made porridge, there were gigantic stodgy lumps in it and that was how he got his name. He didn't like going on boats because if he tried to make soup at sea, it always slopped over the top of the pan. The boiling soup splattered on to his feet and

made him leap about shouting very, VERY
bad words like 'Jigglepops!' and
'Pumplespizz!'

Of course, it was no good having five
pirates without a leader, and Captain
Blackpatch decided that there was only one
possible choice – namely himself. This was
because:

1 It was his house.
2 He said so.
3 He could shout louder than anyone
   else.
4 He liked bossing people about and,
5 See 2.

Blackpatch's first decision was to make
himself Captain. Then he made Lumpy
Lawson the Ship's Cook, Bald Ben his First
Mate, and told the twins he would make
them walk the gangplank if they didn't stop

quarrelling straight away.

The Indoor Pirates did not want anyone to know where they lived, so they took the number off the front door and hung a skull-and-crossbones flag from the chimney-pot instead. All the neighbours knew immediately that they had pirates living near them, but they didn't mind, because the pirates stayed indoors most of the time. (That was how they got their name.)

Old Mrs Bishop, who lived next door, even cut flowers from her garden every so often and gave them to Bald Ben, because

she thought he was rather sweet. Besides, the pirates were not very good at their job.

First of all, since they didn't like the sea, they didn't have a boat. (They had several small boats that they played with in the bath, but they didn't have a proper, full-size pirate boat with an anchor and lots of sails and cannons and ropes.)

They were very fond of their little house, even if it was a bit cramped inside. It only had three bedrooms. The Captain had swiped the biggest – what a surprise! – and that left the twins sharing bunk-beds in one, and Bald Ben and Lumpy Lawson in the other. (Ben had a hammock. He liked to rock himself to sleep.)

The Indoor Pirates liked to think of their house as a ship, even though they weren't at sea, so they had taken out all the stairs and replaced them with rope rigging. Then they had painted all the walls blue with

little white, fluffy clouds
and hung big plastic sea-
gulls from the ceilings.

They worried about
being attacked by other
pirates, so beside each
window they always kept a
good range of weapons:
catapults, swords and
several large buckets of
dishwater. (The pirates all

thought that soaking an enemy with water was THE WORST POSSIBLE THING that they could do to them.)

The Indoor Pirates were very happy at 25 Dolphin Street. For a couple of months everything went swimmingly (even though the twins didn't like swimming), but trouble was never far away.

1 A Visit from the Postman

One morning Captain Blackpatch was
standing in the front room, surrounded by
heaps of clothes. He was very busy doing
the ironing. Normally the Captain was
very good at avoiding the ironing (not to
mention the cooking, cleaning, dusting,
washing, vacuuming and gardening), but
now he was hot,
cross and fed up.

He reckoned he
had been ironing
for at least two
hours and there
was still a
pile as big as an
armchair. He
slammed the

iron down on the table, where it made a big black burn mark and a nasty smell. 'This is ridiculous!' he bellowed. 'Pirates shouldn't have to do ironing. We should have slaves to do our work for us.'

'That's a good idea,' said Polly.

'No, it isn't,' Molly immediately butted in. 'It's a *really* good idea.'

'That's more or less what I said,' Polly shouted.

'Isn't.'

'Is.'

'Isn't.'

'Is.'

'S H U T U P!' roared Captain Blackpatch. 'I have worked out a brilliant plan. We all hide behind the front door and wait for someone to call. When they knock on the door, we leap out and grab them, drag them inside and keep them prisoner. Then,' and here the Captain took a deep

breath before he proudly announced the
next bit, 'we say to them: "You are our
slave and you have to do everything we say
or we'll be very nasty to you!" And they
will be so scared that they'll do anything –
especially the ironing.'

The Indoor Pirates all agreed that this
was an excellent plan and they went and
crouched down behind the front door.
They made quite a heap, all squashed up
together. Bald Ben seemed
worried and at last he
piped up,

'We don't really have to be nasty to them, do we?'

'We're pirates,' grumbled Captain Blackpatch. 'We're supposed to be nasty.'

'I know, I know, but can't we just *say* we're nasty, and not actually *be* nasty?'

Blackpatch heaved a sigh, but before he could answer he was interrupted by the twins quarrelling.

'Stop pushing,' complained Molly.

'I'm not pushing, I'm pulling,' said Polly.

'Stop pulling, then!'

'I'm not. I'm pushing now!'

'Sssh!' said Lumpy, peering through the letter-box. 'Someone is coming up the path.'

The letter-box banged in Lumpy's long face and a letter was stuffed into his mouth, much to his surprise. Captain Blackpatch ignored Lumpy's muffled squeaks and shouted. 'All aboard! Get him!'

The Indoor Pirates leaped up, instantly

fell over each other and sat down again in
such a muddled heap that heads were stuck
between legs, arms appeared to come out
of ears, and the whole lot looked like a
major wrestling disaster. The front door
slowly swung open and the postman stared
down at a wriggling pile of pirates, one of

whom had a letter sticking out of his mouth.

The postman was so astonished that he just stood there. This gave the pirates plenty of time to stagger to their feet. Bald Ben reached out with two brawny arms, picked up the postman and marched into the house. The postman was plonked down on a chair in the back room and the Indoor Pirates crowded round, glaring fiercely at their victim. Lumpy Lawson poked his face right up close to the postman's and bared his teeth threateningly. (He'd taken out the letter.) 'We are your slaves and we will do anything you say!' he hissed.

'No, we're not!' shouted Polly.

'Yes, we are!' cried Molly.

'No, we're not, stupid. We're not *his* slaves. He's *our* slave.'

Captain Blackpatch was hopping from

one foot to the other. 'Jumping jellyfish! Let me do it,' he roared. 'Listen to me, postieperson. You are our slave and you have to do everything we say. Right?' The postman blinked back at them. He took off his

spectacles and began to polish them on his shirt.

'I'm very sorry,' he began, 'but I can't be your slave today because I already have a job as a postman.'

This unexpected reply completely threw the Indoor Pirates, except for Bald Ben, who seemed quite relieved. 'Does that mean we don't have to be nasty to you?' he asked.

'Oh yes, definitely,' nodded the postman, carefully putting his glasses back on. 'I wouldn't recommend any nastiness at all.'

Bald Ben was very pleased to hear this, but Lumpy suddenly gave a howl of horror. He turned deathly white and held out the letter that the postman had just delivered. Lumpy handed it over to Captain Blackpatch, who stared at it, glared at it and then had to sit down in an armchair to get over the shock.

'Whatever is it?' whispered the twins.

'It's the electricity bill,' announced the Captain, just as if he was telling them that the Earth had exploded and everyone was dead. 'Unless we pay up in four weeks, we are going to be cut off.'

'Cut off?' repeated Bald Ben, scratching his tattooed head. 'What does that mean?'

'It means they cut off your legs,' said Polly.

'No,' said Molly, 'it means they cut off your arms.'

'*And* your legs,' insisted Polly. 'And head. And nose. And ears and hair and . . .'

'Excuse me,' said the postman. 'It means that the electricity company will stop supplying the house with electricity unless you pay the bill. If they cut you off, you won't have any lights. You won't be able to cook or watch television or anything.'

'That is just what I was going to say,' growled the Captain. 'How much money has everyone got?'

The Indoor Pirates turned out their pockets and made a pile on the table. Altogether they had one paper-clip, three elastic bands, a lot of fluff, a broken penknife, a very crumpled, signed portrait of Captain Hook and a small heap of coins.

Captain Blackpatch scowled at the pile. 'That's not nearly enough. We need ten times that. Where on earth are we going to find the money?' He stared at the other pirates, and they stared back at him with wild, blank faces.

'THINK!' roared the Captain. 'Think hard!' A deep silence fell on the room. The five pirates paced round and round with strange, twisted expressions on their faces, which showed just how hard they were thinking. At last Blackpatch gave a triumphant shout.

'I've got it! We hold the postman here to ransom! We keep him prisoner and we send a note to the Post Office saying that they must pay us . . . a million pounds, or they will never get their postman back.'

'That's brilliant!' cried Lumpy. 'We shall be rich!'

Even Bald Ben, who was beginning to think that the postman was quite a nice chap, thought it was a good idea. Captain Blackpatch sat down at the table and carefully wrote a ransom demand.

Deer Post Offisss
We hav got your postman.
Giv us a millyon ponds
or you wont get him bak
EVER !!!
Singed: The Indoor Pirates
Bald Ben x x x   Captin Blackpatch
Lumpy Lawson
Molly → Polly
Me not her! ← Me not her!

'Now, all we have to do is send this letter to the Post Office,' chuckled Captain Blackpatch. 'Soon we shall be as rich as kings!'

The postman got to his feet and smiled at everyone. 'As it happens, I was just on my way to the Post Office. I'll take the letter with me if you like.'

Captain Blackpatch was overcome. 'You are kind. What a jolly nice postman you are. Thank you so much. You will deliver it safely, won't you?'

'Of course,' said the postman. 'That's my job.' He took the ransom demand, let himself out by the front door and walked off down the road, whistling cheerfully.

The Indoor Pirates
watched him go and
then hurried into the
front room, where they
sat down by the
window so that they
could see when the
postman was coming
back with the million
pounds.

While they waited,
Lumpy Lawson made everyone a lumpy cup
of tea. (He left the teabags in the cups.)
They drank their tea and they waited.
Lunch-time came and went. Tea-time came
and went. At last Captain Blackpatch got to
his feet.

'I think that postman must have got lost,'
he muttered.

'Some horrible men might have
kidnapped him!' suggested Bald Ben angrily.

27

'What are we going to do about the electricity bill?' moaned Lumpy. 'If I can't use the fridge, half our food will go mouldy.'

Captain Blackpatch started to climb the rope rigging up to his Captain's quarters. 'I can't think any more today,' he grunted. 'I've already had two clever ideas in one day and now I'm worn out. I expect I shall have another clever idea when I wake up tomorrow morning. Obviously nobody else is going to think of anything useful.' He scowled down at his crew. 'I'm going to bed. Batten down the hatches. Good-night!'

'Good-night,' said Molly.

'Good-morning!' said Polly.

2 The Treasure Ship

There was a great deal of clattering on
Dolphin Street. The refuse truck was
slowly making its way down the road. The
dustmen were collecting rubbish from
every house and throwing it into the back
of the truck. The Indoor Pirates had two
sacks of rubbish and Polly carried them to
the back of the truck. 'There's a lot of stuff
in there!' she said. 'I never knew there was
so much rubbish.'

Fred mopped his florid face with a big spotty handkerchief. 'It's amazing what some people throw out,' he said, shaking his head in disbelief. 'This truck is like a treasure chest some weeks.' Polly's eyes almost fell out of their sockets. She tried to appear as calm as possible.

'Oh?' she squeaked. 'Treasure, you say?'

'Every week,' nodded Fred, stuffing his handkerchief inside his baseball cap before shoving it back on his head. 'We get old tellys, foodmixers – all sorts of things that can still be used. We always get lots of tools.'

Just as Fred said 'tools', his mate Tony gave a huge sneeze and drowned his words, but Polly was quite certain that Fred had said 'we always get lots of *jewels*'. She didn't bother to stop and listen to any more. Polly was already half-way up the garden path before Fred had finished counting on his stubby fingers all the treasures: 'old spades, saws, hammers, screwdrivers . . .'

Polly almost smashed the front door off its hinges, she was so excited. She clawed her way up the rigging and barged into the Captain's quarters, where Captain Blackpatch was having breakfast in bed. (Blackpatch had breakfast in bed every Thursday. And also every Tuesday. And also Sundays, Fridays, Mondays, Wednesdays and Saturdays.)

Polly blurted out everything about the refuse truck full of treasure. Blackpatch was rather puzzled at first. He wondered why a rubbish truck should be used for carrying jewels.

'Don't you see?' cried Polly. 'It's a trick! Nobody would ever think of looking in the back of a dustcart for jewels!' Of course, it had to be a trick! Blackpatch grinned from one big ear to the other. Those dustmen were fiendishly clever – fancy hiding jewels in the rubbish!

At this, even Captain Blackpatch got so excited that he spread honey on the back of his teddy. He yelled for the rest of the crew and they came hurrying in. 'Good work, Polly,' said the Captain. 'Prancing prawns, we're going to be rich, lads! We shall be able to pay our electricity bill for the next thousand years!'

'But how are we going to get the

treasure?' asked Bald Ben, hoping very much that it would not involve hitting anybody.

Captain Blackpatch leaped out of bed, even though he wasn't wearing any pyjamas. (He'd gone to sleep in his clothes as usual.) He fixed his crew with a fierce grin. 'We shall wait until the treasure ship sails down our street and then we'll have a boarding party.'

'Hurrah – a boarding party!' shouted Lumpy. 'It's ages since we had a party. I'll make the cakes. I'll do some of those nice chocolatey ones with white icing on the top, and some butterfly-sponges with hundreds and thousands to make them look pretty. I'll bake lots of mini sausage-rolls and put little cubes of cheese on sticks and . . .'

'It's not that kind of party, you dopey doughnut,' roared Captain Blackpatch. 'A boarding party is when we get our swords and we all hang on ropes and go swinging across to the enemy ship and jump on her and take her over and get all the treasure. That's what a boarding party is.'

Lumpy Lawson was crestfallen. 'No cakes or sausage-rolls?' he asked. The other pirates sadly shook their heads. They quite fancied the kind of party Lumpy had just described. However, at least they would get the treasure.

'I'm going to be rich!' said Polly, rubbing her hands.

'No, you're not,' snapped Molly. '*I'm* going to be rich!'

'That's what I said, I'm going to be rich,' Polly repeated.

'No, that's what *I* said. *I'm* going to be rich,' insisted Molly.

'SHUT UP!' bellowed Captain Blackpatch. 'Everybody get your sword. We've got a week before the treasure-ship dustcart-thingummy comes back and we need all the practice we can get so that we are perfect on the day.'

The Indoor Pirates fetched their swords and they practised swinging on ropes and getting into very noisy and dangerous sword fights. They always used wooden swords.

Some while back, they'd had proper metal ones which they tucked into their belts, but every time they pulled out their swords they sliced through their belts and their trousers fell down. Captain Blackpatch decided that wooden swords were a lot better.

They practised day after day. The only

time they stopped was when Bald Ben
discovered his teddy was missing. There
was a dreadful fuss and he just would not
be comforted. Captain Blackpatch offered
Ben his own teddy, although it still had a
rather sticky bottom.

'I don't want your teddy, I want mine,'
wailed Ben. 'I've had him for years and
years and he is my very best friend.'

'Do stop blubbing,' pleaded Molly. 'You
can have my toothbrush that's like a
dinosaur.'

'No, you can have *my* dinosaur

toothbrush,' Polly promised. 'It's bigger
and better than hers.'

It was no use. Bald Ben wanted his teddy
and that was the one thing that could not
be found. They searched the house from
top to bottom, from side to side, and then
front to back. Ben did not stop wailing
until it was bin-day once more and the
Indoor Pirates were getting ready to steal
all the jewels from the refuse truck.

Molly put out two sacks of rubbish next
to the trees on either side of the road. The
pirates grabbed their swords and
clambered up into the leafy branches.
'Wait for my signal,' whispered Blackpatch,
his eyes glinting from between the leaves.
The pirates grasped their ropes.

'Can we have chocolate sponge *after*
this?' mumbled Lumpy Lawson.

'If we get the treasure,' hissed the
Captain, 'you can have a chocolate sponge

as big as a ship. Listen – they're coming!'

With a great clanking and grinding, the refuse truck clattered to a halt between the two trees. Down jumped Fred and Tony to

collect the sacks. They were startled by a
loud yell from the middle of a tree.

'Boarding party – let's get 'em!' And
with swords firmly gripped between their

teeth, the Indoor Pirates swung into action.

Lumpy Lawson forgot to hold his rope and crashed to the ground. 'Oh, fuzzyfigs!'

Bald Ben went zooming straight into the side of the truck, which made his eyes spin round and round as if they were on a spin-cycle.

Molly and Polly landed on the roof of the truck and started to fight each other before they remembered they were on the same side.

Captain Blackpatch swung down beside the driver's cab and dangled at the open window. He glared savagely at Dave the driver. 'Hurfisheruk! Giffusherezzer!'

Dave looked back at the fierce bearded face. 'Beg your pardon?'

'Hurfisheruk! Giffusherezzer!' bellowed Blackpatch.

Dave rested his hairy arms on the steering-wheel. 'If you take that sword out of your mouth I might be able to hear what you are saying,' he suggested calmly. The Captain, who was still holding the rope with both hands, struggled to spit out the sword.

'Splurrrgh! This is our truck!' he snarled. 'Give us the treasure!'

'What treasure?' asked Dave. 'We haven't got any treasure. All we've got is rubbish.'

'Ha!' cried Blackpatch. 'I knew you'd say that! You think I'm stupid, don't you?'

'Yes,' nodded Dave. 'And you are, too.' Fred and Tony nudged each other and grinned.

'You can't fool me,' growled the Captain. 'If you don't give us the treasure, I'll cut off your arms and you'll be swimming in pools of your own blood.'

'No, we won't,' said Dave. 'If you cut off our arms, we won't be able to swim at all.'

'DON'T ARGUE!' thundered Captain
Blackpatch. 'We have boarded your ship
and taken it over. Now, we want the jewels,
and you are going to unload them into our
front garden. GET ON WITH IT!'

The dustmen looked at each other and
shrugged. Tony tugged his cap further
down his weaselly face. 'I always did think
these pirates were a bit daft,' he muttered.

'Better do as they say,' said Fred. 'The
customer is always right.'

Dave frowned at the Captain's sword.
The tip was almost sticking into his nose.
'Stop poking me and I'll back up to your
garden,' he said. The engine hummed and
hurred. The rear of the truck lifted higher
and higher until with a sudden *whoosh!*
out spilled all the rubbish. Within a few
minutes the garden was piled high with a
stinking, messy mountain of muck.

'Help yourselves!' shouted Dave, as Tony

and Fred climbed into the cab alongside
him and they all went off for an early tea-
break.

'Wonderful!' cried Polly.

'It's more than one-derful,' argued Molly.
'It's two-derful.'

'Two-derful?' said Polly. 'What's two-
derful?'

'One more than one-derful, of course,'
Molly answered. 'Two-derful. If it was even

more wonderful it might be three-derful, or even six-derful.'

'You're the most stupid human being in the whole world,' muttered Polly, and she turned back to the stink-pile. The excited pirates pulled out sacks and emptied them. They plunged their arms deep among old fish bones, smelly socks, mouldy cheese wrappers, squidgy tomatoes, soggy pizzas, and hunted for jewels.

'Anyone found anything?' rasped Captain Blackpatch, trying to brush away several thousand flies that seemed to find him very attractive.

'I've got an old hammer,' said Lumpy Lawson.

'I've found a saw,' said Molly.

'I saw the saw first,' Polly began.

'No! I saw the saw you saw first. You saw my saw.'

'QUIET!' boomed the captain. He

straightened his aching back. 'It's no good. Those dustmen must have suspected us right from the start. They've hidden the jewels somewhere else. This is just a filthy pile of rubbish. There's nothing here at all.'

'Oh yes there is!' cried Bald Ben triumphantly. 'Look what I've found – my teddy! He was right at the bottom of the pile!' Ben wiped

a big smear of baked beans from his chin
and his face split into a huge grin. He was
happy at last.

Next door, a window
was flung open and Mrs
Bishop leaned out.
'Captain Blackpatch,' she
said accusingly, 'I do hope
you are not going to leave
that horrible smelly mess
there all week?' And she
glared at the pirates with stern eyes.
Blackpatch gritted his teeth.

'We wouldn't dream of it, Mrs Bishop.
The crew are just about to bag it all up
again.' And while the crew bagged all the
rubbish once more, Blackpatch went inside
and bagged the bathroom.

He ran a deep bath and got in with all
his clothes on. After all, they were just as
dirty as he was. He lay there for an hour,

grumbling and growling to himself, and wondering how they would ever manage to pay that electricity bill. The little plastic boat he had been bombarding with small bits of soap finally sank and Captain Blackpatch closed his eyes. Outside the bathroom, four very smelly pirates patiently waited their turn for a bath.

'You stink,' said Molly.

'*You* stink!' said Polly.

Bald Ben sniffed a couple of times. 'I think we all stink,' he observed ruefully, and they stood and listened to the loud snores coming from the other side of the bathroom door.

3 The Hunt Goes On

Lumpy Lawson was the first to see the notice. He had gone to the shops and was busily using up what little money they had left to buy important supplies – eggs, bacon, chocolate, cereals, chocolate, crisps, fruit, biscuits (chocolate ones), milk and chocolate. And there, in the supermarket window, was the notice.

GRAND EASTER
TREASURE HUNT

COME TO THE PARK
ON SATURDAY!

EVERYONE WELCOME

Lumpy almost dropped the shopping in his haste to get back to 25 Dolphin Street.

He ran all the way there, so by the time he arrived he could barely speak for panting.

'We're going-a-huff-a-huff-a-huff . . .'

Captain Blackpatch, who was busily supervising the housework by lying in an armchair with both eyes closed, opened one fierce eye and glowered at the ship's cook. 'What? What did you say?'

'We're going to be-a-huff-a-huff-a-huff . . .'

'Shivering sharks!' shouted the captain. 'Get a grip on yourself!'

'I'll grip him, Captain,' offered Bald Ben, wrapping his massively muscled arms around Lumpy's body and lifting him completely clear of the ground. Lumpy's arms and legs thrashed about wildly as he tried to breathe. The Captain was beside himself.

'I didn't mean that kind of grip, you big, bald barnacle! Look – he's turning purple.

Let him go at once.'

'Oh – sorry, Captain.' Ben obediently let
go.

Lumpy fell to the floor and so did the
shopping. There was a loud crash and a
large milky puddle appeared beside

Lumpy, quickly joined by some ready-scrambled eggs. Lumpy struggled to his feet. 'We're going to be rich! Everything is going to be all right. There's a Treasure Hunt in the park on Saturday!' And he told the pirates about the poster in the supermarket window.

'Saturday,' said Molly. 'That's tomorrow.'

'No, it isn't,' argued Polly. 'It's the day after today.'

'The day after today *is* tomorrow!'

'It isn't,' insisted Polly. 'The day after today is the day before the day after the day after tomorrow.'

Molly was still trying to puzzle that one out when Captain Blackpatch interrupted. 'We've only got four days left, lads, and then the electricity company are going to cut us off. We've got to get our hands on that treasure in the park tomorrow.'

'What kind of treasure do you think it

might be?' asked Molly. The Captain
tugged at his stormy beard.

'Gold, I expect, and silver too. Maybe
some pearl necklaces and diamond rings.
But we could have a fight on our hands.
Suppose there are other pirates there? The
notice says everyone is welcome. What we
need is a plan, and who makes the best
plans around here?'

The four other pirates looked at each
other, perplexed. Who did make the best
plans? They hadn't got a clue. Captain
Blackpatch tore at his hair.

'I do, you huge hairy half-wits! Now, let
me sit in this nice comfy armchair so that I
can have a proper think.' And he drove the
pirates from the front room with a kick of
one slippered foot.

Lumpy Lawson went stomping back to
the shops to buy some more milk and eggs.
(He got some chocolate too.) Bald Ben

knitted a little cardigan for his teddy bear.
Molly and Polly went upstairs to their
bunk-beds and had a flaming row that
ended with each sister throwing the other's
entire bedding out of the window. This
came as a bit of a surprise to old Mrs
Bishop, who later discovered Polly's pillow
and Molly's night-dress draped over one of
her beautiful rose-bushes.

The following morning, Lumpy made
everyone a lumpy picnic to take with them.

(He made sardine sandwiches with whole sardines.) The pirates grabbed their swords and set off for the park.

'Here we are, lads,' hissed Captain Blackpatch. 'Keep an eye out for pirates.'

The park was certainly full of people, although there didn't seem to be any other pirates. There were a great number of children and a few parents too, but the Indoor Pirates hardly noticed the crowds. They had spotted something so wonderful

that all they could do was fix their eyes on it and sigh deeply.

It was a climbing-frame. It was big, and it was painted bright red and bright green. As if that wasn't enough, the climbing-frame had been built in the shape of a pirate galleon.

'Now, *that's* the kind of ship I like,' said Captain Blackpatch. 'One that's anchored in concrete. Come on, let's seize her!'

The pirates drew their swords and rushed across the play area, yelling and snarling and driving the children from the climbing-frame. The children hurried off to find the park-keeper so that they could complain, while the Indoor Pirates swarmed over their captured prize.

'This is the best ship we've ever had,' grinned Polly.

'It isn't,' said Molly. 'I went on a ship twice as big as this.'

'Well, I went on a ship three times bigger,' Polly butted in.

'My ship had a thousand cannons!' cried Molly.

'My ship had a million cannons,' shouted Polly, 'and its masts reached the sky and its sails were as big as clouds and it could go as fast as a hurricane . . .' she panted. Molly stared back at her sister.

'Well, my ship was even bigger,' she said simply. 'So there.'

Polly drew her sword and was threatening a fight to the death, but Captain Blackpatch had had enough and he ordered her up to the top of the mast to act as look-out, and a good thing too. Hardly had Polly taken up position when she gave a cry of alarm. 'Pirate on the starboard bow, Captain!' she cried.

Sure enough, a large, red-faced park-keeper with big boots and bristling moustache was marching straight towards them, surrounded by an excited gaggle of children. 'Look here,' he complained. 'You big pirates can't play here. This is for children.'

'I like your hat,' said Lumpy Lawson admiringly. 'Can I have it?'

'Of course not. This hat is the property of the Parks and Gardens Department.' The park-keeper wagged a large and menacing finger at the pirates. 'Now, get off at once!'

There was no way that the Indoor Pirates were going to have their newly won ship taken away from them. Captain Blackpatch whispered something in Bald Ben's ear.

'Raaargh!' snarled Ben, suddenly leaping overboard. The children screamed and scattered like frightened shrimps, while Ben seized the surprised park-keeper, tucked him under his arm and returned to the ship.

'Well done!' whooped Captain Blackpatch. 'Our first prisoner. Tie him to the gangplank over there!' And he jabbed a finger towards the slide. Bald Ben carried the struggling park-keeper to the top of the slide and tied him firmly to the railings.

(Lumpy Lawson had whipped his hat and was proudly wearing it.) The poor park-keeper shouted at the children, pleading to be rescued, but the children had better things to do. The Great Treasure Hunt had started.

All over the park excited children were rushing about, finding Easter eggs. They were hidden under bushes. They were taped to tree branches, and the children gathered them from their hiding-places, clutching the shiny foil-wrapped eggs in their arms. Polly gave another excited yell.

'I spy treasure!' she cried, her round eyes fixed on the shiny eggs. 'I spy huge jewels and masses of them!'

The Indoor Pirates were astonished. Never had they seen such wonderful rubies and sapphires and emeralds! 'Ha! We're going to be rich after all!' yelled Blackpatch, drawing his sword. 'Raiding party – follow me!'

Round the park went the pirates, poking and prodding with their swords and gathering jewels wherever they went. The children ran off crying and the pirates ran off with their arms bulging with booty. They went back to the ship and piled up their treasures. They sat round the heap and picked up the jewels one by one.

'My ruby is worth a trillion pounds,' sighed Polly.

'My emerald is worth more than the Bank of England,' Molly claimed.

'And mine is worth more than all the banks in the world,' said Polly.

Molly glanced mischievously at her sister. 'Mine is worth the most,' she said, 'because I've got yours!' Molly made a sudden grab for Polly's ruby egg. 'Oh!' they both cried, as the jewel crumbled into little pieces. Bits of chocolate tumbled out from the split foil wrapper.

For a few moments, the pirates stared at

the broken jewel, then all at once they began scrummaging through their treasures. 'They're all the same!' roared Captain Blackpatch. 'We've been diddled. These aren't jewels – they're chocolate eggs!'

Lumpy Lawson stuck a piece in his mouth and sucked on it happily. 'Oh well, it could be worse,' he pointed out, and he was right, because at that very moment a tidal wave of furious children swept over them.

The robbed children had gone off to find the park-keeper again and when they found him tied to the top of the slide, they quickly released him. Now they were on the war-path. Fifty-seven children, a large, red (hat-less) park-keeper, three dogs and a pony (which had run away from giving pony rides) rushed up and threw themselves upon the pirates.

'Give us back our eggs!'

'Down with the pirates!'

It was the biggest, noisiest, biff-and-bammiest fight that the park had ever seen, and the pirates got by far the worst of it.

'Ouch!' (That was Bald Ben.)

'Eeeek!' (That was Polly.)

'I said Eeeek first!' (That was Molly.)

'Bumbleflip!' (That was Lumpy Lawson.)

Dust and grass flew everywhere. Arms whirled round, mostly with fists on them. Legs scrabbled in the dirt. Easter

eggs came whizzing out from the middle of this human hurricane, and so did several lumpy sardine sandwiches and a park-keeper's hat, much to everyone's surprise.

At last, all the heaving and wriggling and shouting stopped. The children gathered up their rather battered eggs and marched away happily. The park-keeper went off to try and get all the dents out of his hat, and that just left the Indoor Pirates, somewhere inside an enormous cloud of dust.

The dust slowly settled and there they were, all tied up in one big heap. 'I want to go home,' sniffed Ben. Captain Blackpatch was wondering why it had got dark so early. (Someone had rammed his hat down over his eyes.)

They sat there for a very long time, until at last the Captain realized that nobody was going to come and untie them. After several efforts, they managed to stand up. They set off for home, waddling up the road like some weird ten-legged beastie from the bottom of the sea. Blackpatch couldn't see where he was going.

'This way!' cried Polly.

'THIS way!' yelled Molly.

'Stop tugging!'

'I'm not tugging, I'm clugging,' said Molly.

'There's no such thing as clugging!'

'Yes, there is. It's what you do when

you're not tugging.' Molly gave such a tug
against her sister that all five of them fell
over and began rolling across the grass.

'This is ridiculous!' roared Captain
Blackpatch. 'What's going on? Where are
we? I've just about had enough of you

twins! Splurrgh!' He spat a large clump of grass from his mouth and the pirates rolled merrily on. It was a miracle that they got back home at all.

4 A Few House Alterations

The twins were arguing AGAIN, busily hitting each other with their pillows. 'You always have the top bunk,' snarled Polly.

'No, I don't!' shouted Molly, giving her sister such a slosh round the head that her

pillow burst and the room was filled with
tiny white feathers. 'You've had the top
bunk all this week.'

'And you had it all last month!' Polly
cried.

'Well, you had it all last year – and the
year before that and the year before that
and the year before that . . .'

'You had it last all century!' screamed
Polly, trying to smother her sister's face
with her pillow. 'You had it before we were
even born!'

'Stop – S T O P!' thundered the
Captain, 'before I make you
both walk the plank. I
won't have any more of
this. I can't bear it
any longer.'

Bald Ben waved a
thick hairy arm in
the air. (Luckily it

was his.) 'I've got a good idea.' The other
pirates stopped in their tracks and stared at
him. Bald Ben had an idea? Ben never had
ideas. Ben was kind, Ben was strong and
Ben was helpful – but he didn't have ideas.

Ben grinned back at the others. 'Why
don't we take the bunk-beds apart? We
could put one bed on each side of the
bedroom and then there won't be any
bunks to argue about.'

Captain Blackpatch was impressed.
'You're a clever lad, Ben, have one of my
fruit gums. Take a yellow one, I don't like
them.'

Everybody went upstairs and watched
while Ben did all the lifting himself, even
though it made his face look like boiled
beetroot. The beds were separated and put
on either side of the little room.

'There,' said the Captain. 'Let's see you
quarrel about that.'

Polly threw herself triumphantly on one of the beds. 'This is mine!' she cried, daring Molly to say that it wasn't. Molly smiled sweetly and sauntered across to the other bed.

'This is mine,' she agreed, and the Indoor Pirates smiled with relief. 'Because it's better than Polly's bed and it's the best bed in the whole world!'

Polly was on her feet in an instant, eyes blazing. 'Mine's the best bed in the galaxy – no, in the universe!' Blackpatch almost exploded. His eyes became narrow, furious slits. His mouth turned into such a snarl that all his teeth could be seen, glinting like daggers. He drew his sword and was advancing menacingly on the twins, when Bald Ben waved his hairy arm again.

'I've had another idea!' he shouted. The pirates groaned. This was almost becoming a habit. 'Let's put one of the beds downstairs, then Polly and Molly won't be able to see each other at night.'

'Excellent idea, Ben,' said Captain Blackpatch. 'Have another yellow fruit gum.'

Unfortunately, try as they might, the Indoor Pirates could not get Polly's bed out through the door. They even tried the window, but that was unsuccessful too. Eventually they gave up and the Captain stomped off in a huff, complaining that the real problem was that their house was too small. 'Three bedrooms aren't enough,' he grumbled.

'You've got a room all of your own,' said

Lumpy peevishly. 'We all have to share. You're the only one with a room of your own.'

Captain Blackpatch turned very red and quickly changed the subject. 'We are about to have our electricity cut off. Do you understand how serious that is? What we need is treasure. If we had treasure we could pay our electricity bill and . . .' Blackpatch grinned craftily. 'We could buy a bigger house, with five bedrooms.'

The other pirates liked the sound of this new house, but treasure was difficult to find. It wasn't the sort of thing that was just left lying around, and that was why Lumpy Lawson was so surprised when he discovered a treasure map in the kitchen cupboard. He had been looking for something useful, like chocolate biscuits, when he found the map stuck to the bottom of the marmalade jar.

(Actually, it wasn't a map at all. Long before the Indoor Pirates had moved into Number 25, Great-granny Blackpatch had needed a new front gate. She had written down the measurements on a scrap of paper: 75 centimetres wide, 90 centimetres high and 5 centimetres deep.)

'Look – a treasure map!' shouted Lumpy, and he carefully spread the map on the

kitchen table. The other pirates wrinkled their noses and wondered what it all meant.

Captain Blackpatch tugged hard at his beard, his eyebrows knitting together in a fierce frown. 'It's directions,' he growled. 'It means start at the gate.' The pirates crowded round excitedly. A real treasure map! Their eyes grew shiny and their mouths fell open, which was a little unfortunate because Bald Ben began to dribble. (He nearly always dribbled when he thought about gold and jewels and coins.)

'What's 75 W?' asked Polly.

'Don't you know?' Molly sneered.

'Tell us, then,' Polly dared her sister.

'It means . . . woodlice!' cried Molly, saying the first thing she could think of that began with a 'w'.

'Seventy-five woodlice!' snarled Captain

Blackpatch. 'What kind of treasure is that?
It's W for West. That's what it means.
75 West.'

'What about 90 h?' asked Ben.

'It's not an 'h', it's an 'n' for North.
90 North,' said Captain Blackpatch, 'and
then it's 5 down. Start at the gate, 75 paces
West, 90 paces North and dig down 5 paces.
Come on – let's go!'

The pirates took the instructions for a
front gate, grabbed some spades and
shovels and rushed out to the front garden.
'This way!' cried Blackpatch, consulting his
compass. The pirates tramped across the
garden, climbed in through their own
window and marched West across the front
room. Then they went North through to
the kitchen, still counting, into the back
garden, over the wall and into Mrs
Bishop's beautiful garden next door.

'88, 89, 90!' cried the Captain, standing

in the middle of a rather splendid flower-bed. 'Start digging.'

Plants and mud and garden gnomes began flying everywhere. The hole got deeper and deeper and Mrs Bishop's flowers flew higher and higher as the pirates dug up every single one. 'Anybody found anything?' asked the Captain impatiently.

'I've got some worms,' said Molly.

'I've got more worms than you,' Polly muttered.

'I've got an old shoe,' cried Bald Ben.

'Oh, it's mine!'

'I've got backache,' grumbled Lumpy.

At that moment, a terrible scream came
from the house and Mrs Bishop
came rushing out on her walking-
frame as fast as she could
manage. 'Aargh! What are
you doing to my wonderful
garden? You stupid, stupid
pirates! Get out at once!'
She was so angry she
seized her walking-frame
and hurled it at the rapidly
retreating pirates.

'Ouch!' cried Bald Ben as
it bounced off his bottom.

The pirates scrambled
back over the wall, rushed inside, locked
the back-door and pulled the curtains.
'Phew,' sighed Lumpy. 'That was a narrow
escape.'

'Not for me it wasn't,' muttered Ben, rubbing his rear. The Captain was re-examining the crumpled map.

'I don't think we counted right,' he said, 'It can't mean paces. It must mean feet. Come on, back to the gate.'

The pirates tramped outside and started again, even though it was beginning to get dark. The Captain carefully counted every step. '88, 89, 90. Now, dig.' The Indoor Pirates eyed their great leader.

'But, Captain, we're in the middle of our own back room.'

'So is the treasure then!' cried Blackpatch. 'Dig!'

They set to right away. Out of the window went the furniture. Up came the carpet and the floor-boards. The pirates began digging and very shortly there was a deep hole and an ever-increasing pile of rubble all round the edge.

'I've hit something!' cried Lumpy
Lawson. 'Look!'

Captain Blackpatch scrambled down
into the hole and brushed dirt away from
the object, until he revealed a large, black,
metal box. A breathless silence filled the
small room. 'Look, lads,' whispered the
Captain, his eyes shining
like diamonds. 'It's the
treasure. We've found
the treasure. Our
troubles are over!
Hand me that
pickaxe, Molly,
and let's see
what's in
store for us!'

Blackpatch seized the pickaxe, raised it
high above his head and brought it
smashing down on the big black treasure
chest.

What an explosion! Enormous crackling sparks sizzled and spat from the box. The Indoor Pirates were hurled into the air, where they bounced off the ceiling before crashing back down into the hole, one on top of the other. Bricks and plaster, dust and floor-boards and shreds of carpet roared around the room in a violent whirlwind, clattering and battering at the poor pirates.

Great cracks shot up the walls and went zigzagging across the ceiling. They splintered in every direction, split open and widened. Then, just as the pirates were thinking that the world had come to an end, a great, gaping hole opened in the ceiling and Polly's bed fell through and landed on their heads.

'OW!' yelled all five at once, before collapsing back at the bottom of the smoking pit.

All along Dolphin Street the neighbours came rushing out of their houses to see why all their lights, all the street lights and half the town's lights had suddenly gone out. They looked across at Number 25.

The windows had burst from their frames. The front door was hanging on one hinge. The chimney-pot (along with a very tattered skull-and-crossbones) had been hurled high into the sky before smashing into smithereens on the road below. Tiles slid slowly down the roof, sliced through the air and then crashed into the gardens, front and back.

Deep inside Number 25 the big black box smouldered, and black, choking smoke poured from the broken casing. Molly poked it with a grimy foot. 'That's not a treasure chest,' she coughed angrily. 'That was an electricity junction box and we've just cut off our own electricity.'

'Yes, it is, and we have,' nodded Polly and the twins stared in horror at each other. They had actually agreed on something!

Bald Ben sniffed loudly. 'I don't like it when it's dark,' he moaned. 'It's scary and I've got a nasty bang on my head where Polly's bed fell on me and a bruise on my bottom and there's something sharp sticking in my back and I'm probably going to die.'

Lumpy Lawson crawled across to his friend. 'Lean forward so that I can see,' he said, peering at Ben's back. 'It's all right – you're not going to die. You were lying on

this old tin.' Lumpy pulled a small,
battered tin from the rubble. As he did, the
lid fell off and out tumbled a thick wad of
paper with an elastic band round it.

'Money!' screamed Captain Blackpatch,
seizing the wad and breaking the band.
'Money! Money! Money!' He threw the
hundred-pound notes into the air and they
rained gently down upon the soot-covered
pirates. 'Great-granny must have hidden
this away years ago! We're rich, lads! We

can pay the electricity bill and repair all
this damage, and buy . . .'

'. . . an enormous chocolate sponge-cake?'
suggested Lumpy hopefully.

'Definitely an enormous chocolate
sponge-cake,' agreed the Captain.

Bald Ben began to giggle. 'Look, we've
even got Polly's bed downstairs.' And he
pointed at the rather dented bed that was
lying on its side. Polly put it the right way
up and stretched out on it. 'I'm sleeping
downstairs tonight,' she said wearily.

'And I'm sleeping upstairs,' yawned Molly, both of them too exhausted to argue any longer.

Captain Blackpatch rested back against a pile of rubble and gave a deeply satisfied sigh. He picked up a few hundred-pound notes. 'Money at last,' he murmured. 'And do you know, I think we have found something even better to treasure.'

The Indoor Pirates looked at their leader. What was he talking about? Blackpatch grinned at them through the

dusty gloom of the exploded room. 'Listen –
what can you hear? Nothing. That is the
sound of silence. Molly and Polly have
stopped quarrelling. Now that really *is*
something to treasure!'

Jeremy Strong

The Indoor Pirates on
Treasure Island

Illustrated by Nick Sharratt

This is for Jack

Contents

1 An Introduction to the Indoor Pirates

There were lots of things the Indoor Pirates didn't like. They didn't like the sea, because it was wet. They didn't like the rain, because that was wet too. And they didn't like bathing much, because that was very, VERY wet.

They didn't even like going on boats because they got collywobbles in their stomachs. (But they did like playing with boats in the bath.) It was because they didn't like the sea or boats that they lived in a house, and that was why they were called the Indoor Pirates – because they lived indoors, of course, at number 25 Dolphin Street.

There were five pirates altogether, with Captain Blackpatch as the leader. He had a thin pointy beard, a thin pointy moustache, and a thin pointy nose. He had a proper black patch too, even though it was on the torn sleeve of his jacket and not over one eye like most pirate captains. Captain Blackpatch reckoned he was a very good captain, and he gave

orders to his crew in a gruff, captain-ing
kind of voice. Then he'd sneak off and have
a little nap while everyone else worked.

There were two girl pirates, and their
names were Molly and Polly. They were
twins and they spent most of their time
arguing with each other. They could argue
about absolutely anything, and they would
too. Molly might say, 'I can run faster than
you.'

And Polly would say,
'So? SO?! I can run
slower than you!'

That was just the sort
of silly quarrel they liked to
have. On and on they'd go, arguing about
their hair, or how prongy their forks were,
or how much fizz they had in their drink –
until Captain Blackpatch got so cross he'd
make them walk the plank. Even then Polly
and Molly carried on arguing.

'You go first.'

'No – *you* go first.'

'I'll go first if you go in front of me!'

Eventually Blackpatch would get so fed up with listening to them, he would put on his earphones and turn up his Walkman. (Captain Blackpatch liked listening to *101 Sea Songs for Landlubbers*.)

Bald Ben was First Mate. He had huge muscles and was so strong he could lift up an armchair with one arm. (I don't mean the armchair had one arm – I mean Bald Ben only needed one arm to lift it up.) Bald Ben wasn't totally bald. He did have *something* on his head, and that was a tattoo of a red rose. Underneath the rose was a message: I LOVE MUM.

The fifth Indoor Pirate was Lumpy Lawson. He was tall and thin and he was Chief Cook and Scrubber-Upper. Sadly, he was not terribly good at cooking. Lumpy Lawson's gravy had more lumps in it than a bag of potatoes. When he got upset about something he also had a habit of shouting out very bad words, like 'jigglepoops!'

Although they didn't like boats or the sea, the pirates had made the inside of their house just like a boat. There were no stairs, just rope rigging to climb up and down. They had painted the walls blue with fluffy white clouds. There were several plastic seagulls hanging from the ceilings.

The pirates thought that living in a house was much better than being on a boat. For one thing, they could go to the shops and the park whenever they wanted. The Indoor

Pirates liked going to the park because there was a big climbing frame there built in the shape of a pirate ship. They didn't get seasick when they went on this pirate ship, and if it rained they could run home before they got too wet.

Of course, the Indoor Pirates tried to pretend they weren't pirates at all. It was

supposed to be a secret, but everyone knew because there was a big black Jolly Roger flying from the chimney pot of number 25 and, in any case, they dressed like pirates. The milkman knew straight away.

'You're a pirate, aren't you?' he asked Captain Blackpatch.

'No, I'm not!'

'Yes you are. You're wearing a pirate

captain's hat and pirate clothes. You must be a pirate.'

'No I'm not!' growled Captain Blackpatch.

'What are you then?'

'I'm . . . I'm . . . I'm a bank manager!' declared Blackpatch.

'A bank manager! Don't be silly. Bank managers don't wear pirate costumes.'

'We're having a fancy dress party at the bank,' the Captain claimed rather lamely.

'Oh yes?' The milkman raised his eyebrows. 'And my name's Snow White.'

Captain Blackpatch gazed back haughtily. 'I think that's a very silly name for a milkman,' he said, snatching two pints of milk from the milkman and slamming the door.

Despite all the pretence, the neighbours quite liked the pirates. Mrs Bishop, who lived at number 27, was especially fond of Bald Ben. He often carried her shopping bags home for her. Sometimes she cut flowers from her garden and gave them to him, and sometimes she made all the pirates little cakes and biscuits. The pirates loved Mrs Bishop's cakes and biscuits because they didn't have lumps in them, unlike the ones Lumpy Lawson made.

Life at number 25 Dolphin Street had been going along fairly smoothly for some time, until the day Captain Blackpatch went into town because he had run out of jelly babies. He bought some more without any trouble, but he missed the bus back from the shops, and had to wait over an hour, *in the rain*, and came back soaked to the skin.

He stood in the hall with water dripping from his hat, his nose, his hair, his beard, his arms and all his clothes. A large pool of water collected around his feet. 'The bus never came!' he roared. 'I could have got home more quickly if I'd walked!'

'Why didn't you?' asked Lumpy Lawson, and a very sensible question it was too.

Blackpatch ignored him. He pulled off his coat and wrung it out. 'I shall tell you one thing – I am never going to wait for a bus again, and I am never going to stand in the rain like that again either.'

'That's two things,' said Bald Ben. 'You

said you'd only tell us one thing. Which of those two things do you want us to listen to?'

Captain Blackpatch shot a murderous glance at him, but Bald Ben was much stronger than he was so he decided not to murder him after all. 'And,' the Captain went on, 'I am going to learn to drive.'

'That's three things . . .' Bald Ben began.

'Stop arguing with me! You're even worse than Molly and Polly!'

'No he's not,' said Polly.

'No he is,' said Molly. 'He's the worstest . . . er . . . the worsting worserer . . . I mean the worsingest . . . Oh bother, I give up!'

Captain Blackpatch jumped on to the table, drew his wooden sword and waved it at them threateningly. 'Wobbling walruses! Will you listen? I am going to learn to drive a car. Then we shan't need to wait for buses any longer and we can go just where we like. Tomorrow morning, when I am nice and dry, we shall go to the garage and buy a car.'

   And that is exactly what they did. The garage man was a little scared when he found himself surrounded by pirates, but he was glad to get rid of one of his rather battered vehicles. Captain Blackpatch fixed his eyes on a small truck. It was blood red, which was an excellent pirate colour, and it had a cabin at the front big enough for two people, and an open space at the back for carrying loads, a bit like the deck of a boat.

   'That will do nicely,' said the Captain,

turning to the garage man. 'How many cannons does it have?'

'Cannons?' The garage man shook his head. 'What do you want cannons for?'

'For battles, of course.'

'I think you'll find that other trucks don't have cannons, so I'm sure you'll be all right.'

'Hmmmm. Well, I shall only buy it if you paint a skull and crossbones on each door, *and* I want a Jolly Roger flying from the aerial. It needs an anchor as well.'

'An anchor?'

'Yes, an anchor so that I can make it stop.'

'But it's got new brakes,' explained the garage man.

'I don't think you heard me,' growled the Captain. 'I won't buy it without the skull and crossbones, a pirate flag, *and* an anchor.'

The garage man sighed and said he'd find an anchor. He also arranged to deliver the truck to the house since Blackpatch couldn't actually drive yet. In the meantime, the Indoor Pirates went home so that the Captain could arrange his first driving lesson.

'When we go out in the truck,' said Polly, 'I'm going to sit in the front.'

'You'll have to sit on *me* then,' snarled Molly, 'because I'm getting in the front before you.'

The Captain drew his sword and said that nobody was going to sit up front, except him. 'You lot can all sit in the back,' he declared.

'But we might get wet,' Bald Ben pointed out.

'Good. Maybe it will make your hair grow,' snapped Blackpatch, and then picked up the telephone so that he could arrange some driving lessons. Although he sounded rather grumpy, he was secretly looking forward to driving his pirate truck.

2 A Testing Time

The next day Mr Crock the driving
instructor knocked at number 25. When
Blackpatch opened the front door, Mr
Crock took one look and jumped back a
step. 'Goodness me, you're a pirate!'

'No I'm not,' scowled Blackpatch. 'I'm a
bank manager.'

The instructor burst out laughing. 'If
you're a bank manager my
name's Snow White!'

'Don't be stupid,'
grunted the Captain.
'The milkman's Snow
White. Now, teach me
how to drive.'

The Indoor Pirates
went rushing outside and
leaned over the garden

wall cheering while Mr Crock and the
Captain climbed into the truck. The engine
rattled and roared. The exhaust pipe sent
out a puff of blue smoke and burped very
loudly.

'It *has* got a cannon!' cried Captain
Blackpatch with delight, as the other pirates
dived for cover and fell higgledy-piggledy
on top of each other. 'I heard it go bang!'

'I think it backfired,' murmured Mr
Crock.

'Don't be daft. Cannons can't backfire.
You might be a driving instructor but I
don't think you're very bright. Do you know

what would happen if cannons *did* backfire? We'd end up shooting ourselves. What's the point in doing that?'

Mr Crock didn't have an answer to this, so he meekly suggested that they got going.

'Full speed ahead!' cried Captain Blackpatch and off they went,

with a *jolt*,

and a *judder*,

and a *jerk*,

and a *jump*.

The driving instructor clung to his seat as Captain Blackpatch went sailing down the road at an ever-increasing speed. The first corner was coming up fast.

'I think now would be a good time to try an emergency stop,' shouted Mr Crock.

'OK – anchors away!' shouted the Captain and he hurled the anchor out through the window so that it hooked round a passing lamp-post.

Unfortunately, the anchor was attached to the rear bumper, and as soon as the chain was paid out there was a sickening KERRUNCH! and the bumper was torn off the back. The truck went careering on and there was a second sickening KERRUNCH! – as it finally managed to stop by ploughing straight into a rather stout and sturdy tree.

After that first little drive, Captain Blackpatch had to wait a week for his next lesson because the truck was in the garage, recovering from its bruises, and Mr Crock was in bed at home, recovering from *his* bruises.

When Blackpatch did have another lesson, Mr Crock started by carefully showing his pirate-pupil the brake and explaining what it was, what it did, and how to use it. From then on, the Captain's driving improved rapidly and soon Mr Crock decided that Captain Blackpatch was ready to take his driving test.

'You'd better get your friends to help you learn the Highway Code,' he suggested.

The Indoor Pirates enjoyed testing the Captain. Their glorious leader sat on a chair in the middle of the room, surrounded by the crew who fired questions at him very fiercely, as if he was their prisoner and they were trying to find out where the hidden treasure was.

'What should you always do before you start driving?' asked Molly.

'Switch the engine on.'

'No, something else.'

'Shut the door.'

'No, something else,' insisted Molly.

'Er, take off the handbrake?'

'No, something else . . .'

'Blow your nose?'

'No, something –'

'I DON'T KNOW!' exploded Captain Blackpatch. 'Tell me, you idiot!'

'Look in your mirror, signal, then pull out.'

'Why should I look in my mirror? To see if my lipstick's on properly? I'm not a girly!'

Polly pointed at her twin sister. 'You're a girly!'

'Yeah – and you're a boyly!' sneered Molly.

'A boyly! What's a boyly meant to be?' Polly demanded.

'It's what you are,' snapped Molly, who hadn't got a clue what she was talking about – and neither had anyone else.

'What does a triangular sign mean with a picture of a cow?' asked Bald Ben.

'Low-flying cows.'

'Wrong!' shouted Bald Ben happily. 'Now you have to start again.' Ben made it sound as if they were playing snakes and ladders.

Captain Blackpatch got to his feet. 'I'm not putting up with any more of this,' he sulked. 'I'm going to bed. Nobody around here seems to appreciate who's been putting in all the work. I have been learning to drive, and with good reason because I have got a plan. In fact, it's more of a treat than a plan. If I fail my test tomorrow then you'll all be sorry. So there.'

And Blackpatch clambered up the rope rigging to his bedroom, leaving the other pirates wondering what sort of treat their captain had in mind.

Captain Blackpatch was very surprised when he met the driving-test examiner. 'You're a woman!' he cried.

Mrs Broadside ticked a little box on her examination sheet. 'Well done,' she murmured. 'You have just passed the eyesight test. Shall we go? What should you do first, before you start?'

'Er, check my lipstick.'

'I beg your pardon?'

'I mean, mirror, signal and move off.'

'Good. Off we go then. What an interesting vehicle. I like the skull and crossbones.' Mrs Broadside glanced at the Captain. 'You must be a pirate.'

'No, I'm a bank manager.'

'Really? I suppose it's much the same thing. Now, how about a three-point turn.'

Captain Blackpatch's three-point turn actually had four-and-a-half points in it, but Mrs Broadside didn't seem to mind, and only shut her eyes briefly. Nor did Mrs Broadside seem to mind when the Captain reversed into a pillar box and knocked it over. Mrs Broadside shut her eyes for several seconds and gave her head a little shake.

She didn't even seem worried when she asked the Captain what the speed limit on the High Street was, and he thought she wanted him to drive along it as fast as possible. They raced down the High Street at eighty-five miles an hour. This time, Mrs Broadside kept her eyes shut all the time and Captain Blackpatch was sure she was singing to herself – or maybe it was a little moan.

'Emergency stop!' cried Mrs Broadside, and Blackpatch threw the anchor out of the window. This time, it was not the bumper that came off, but the lamp-post that was wrenched from the ground and dragged behind with a lot of clanging and clattering.

They went back to the test centre where Mrs Broadside sat inside the truck, in silence, with her eyes still shut, for what seemed like ages. Captain Blackpatch pushed the battered

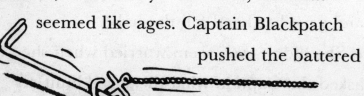

lamp-post to one side and bit his lip nervously. Had he passed? At last Mrs Broadside took a deep, deep breath, opened her eyes and turned to the Captain.

'Mr Blackpatch, if I fail you on this test you will probably come back and frighten the living daylights out of me all over again. I don't want that to happen, so I am going to pass you, on one condition . . .'

'I am yours for ever, delightful woman!' cried Blackpatch in an enthusiastic display of relief.

'Go away! I don't want you to be mine for one second, let alone for ever. I will pass you only on the condition that if you ever see me again you will drive away in the opposite direction. Is that understood?'

'If you insist.'

Mrs Broadside did insist. She got out of the truck and staggered into the test centre. Captain Blackpatch gave her a cheerful toot and drove back home. He screeched to a halt outside number 25 and leaped out of the truck.

'I won!' he yelled, jigging a little hornpipe up the path.

The other pirates came hurtling out of the house and crowded round their leader. 'Oh good,' shouted Bald Ben. 'Well done, Cap'n.'

Molly and Polly tugged at their gallant leader. 'Then we can have a treat after all.

What is it?' Captain Blackpatch grinned at their expectant faces.

'We are going on a holiday,' he announced.

'A holiday!' cried Lumpy Lawson. 'I've never had a holiday before.'

'Yes, a camping holiday,' added Blackpatch, 'with a proper tent and everything. It will be terrific.'

Blackpatch was only slightly wrong here. As things turned out, the holiday was not exactly 'terrific', but it was something beginning with 't-e-r-r', and it did have the same number of letters. But it was a word that meant something a lot different.

3 Trouble from Next Door

The campsite was large, and full of campers. There were big tents and little tents. There were trailer tents and tents on wheels. There were tents that looked like igloos and tents that looked like tepees . . . and then there was the Indoor Pirates' tent, and that looked like nothing on earth.

The pirates had never put up a tent before. Captain Blackpatch stood on the deck of the truck and shouted out instructions. 'That pole goes there, Lumpy. No, not in Ben's ear, you hopeless haddock! Down a bit . . . up a bit . . .'

But it was no use. Nobody really knew what they were

doing, not even the Captain. By the time they had finished, the tent was flat in one place and pointy in another. It was floppy in the middle and stretchy round the edges. It had a door in the roof and a plastic window

on the floor. Even Lumpy Lawson thought there were a few too many lumps in it. 'I don't think we've put it up properly,' he said.

'Why is the window on the bottom?' asked Polly. 'That's silly.'

'No it isn't,' Molly replied. 'That's so we can say "hello" to all the worms and things.'

'Nobody says "hello" to worms! You're stupid.'

'I'm not. You have to say "hello" to them, otherwise they'll think you're rude and they'll bite you.'

'Worms don't bite.'

'They'll bite *you*,' insisted Molly. 'They always bite horrible people, and they'll suck out all your bones and your body will go like jelly and you'll be all floppy and everyone will laugh at you and call you things like Polly-wobble and –'

'Pickled penguins!' roared Blackpatch.

'We are trying to put up a tent. We are not having a discussion about being polite to worms. I've had enough. I am going exploring to see where everything is, and by the time I come back I expect this tent to be put up properly.'

Blackpatch left the other pirates to get on with the hard work, while he went for a gentle stroll. His head was all in a bother and he needed a bit of peace and quiet so that it could un-bother itself.

It was an interesting campsite, full of twisty paths that wound their way among the many tents and caravans. Blackpatch hardly noticed, but as he strode along people popped out of their tents and pointed and whispered to each other. 'Pirates! There are pirates on the campsite!'

The Captain reached the far end of the camp, and there he made a very important discovery. The campsite was built next to a lake. It was a big blue lake, shimmering in the late-afternoon sun, but it was not the lake itself that caught the Captain's attention. It was what was in the middle of the lake.

There was an island – a small, wooded island. A hill crowned the middle, and a little beach ran all around its edge like a rim around a hat.

Now, although Captain Blackpatch didn't care for the sea, or lakes, or ponds, or puddles, or even little *drips* of water, he *did* like islands. As far as Captain Blackpatch knew there was only one reason for there being an island. Islands were there so that people could bury things on them. And the only things that people buried were valuable things – like treasure.

Looking across the shining water, Blackpatch could see people on the distant island. What were they doing? Surely they were digging? DIGGING! He screwed up his eyes and squinted hard, trying to focus them more clearly. The big question was: were the diggers putting something in, or taking something out?

A little boy ran past, stopped, came back slowly and then stood and stared at the Captain. 'Are you a *real* pirate?' he asked. Blackpatch glared down at him fiercely.

'I might be. Are those real binoculars hanging round your neck?' The boy nodded. 'In that case, I'm a real pirate and if you don't lend them to me I'll chop you up and make you into sausages.'

The boy, whose name was Jack, didn't budge, but merely asked what kind of sausages. 'Pork and herb, or spicy beef?'

Captain Blackpatch grabbed the binoculars. 'Don't be so cheeky! You children are supposed to be scared of pirates. Haven't you seen Captain Hook in that film?'

'Yes, an' the crocodile got him and it'll get you too. Give me my binoculars back.' Jack made a grab for his binoculars.

'Don't snatch, you horribly small, squeaky person. Urgh! Half your front teeth are missing!'

'They came out and there are new ones growing. I bet you don't get new teeth when yours fall out, 'cos you're too old. Give me my binoculars or I'll tell my mum.'

'Will you stop snatching? I must see what they're doing on the island. I don't care if you tell the Queen Mother. I'm not scared of wimpy-pimpy women. Ah! Brilliant! They

132

are burying something! We're going to be rich!' Blackpatch at last let go of the binoculars and Jack ran off.

The Captain hurried back to the tent and was surprised to find it looking just as it should. The door was in the right place, and so were the window, the ceiling, and the

floor. Lumpy Lawson had set up a barbecue. Bald Ben was gathering a little bunch of wild flowers but, best of all, there was no sign of the twins.

'They had an argument about who could run the furthest,' said Lumpy Lawson. 'They set off to find out and haven't come back yet. Oh, pimplepox! The flames have gone out again.'

'The lady next door put the tent up for us,' explained Bald Ben. 'She's ever so nice. I think she likes me.' Bald Ben's face cracked into a huge grin and he flushed red. 'She said I was just like a big baby.'

Blackpatch was about to point out to Ben that being called a big baby was not exactly a compliment, but he had far more important things to say. 'Come closer,' he whispered. 'Don't tell anyone, but I think there's treasure near by.'

'Treasure!' cried Bald Ben.

'Ssssh! I said don't tell *anyone*. There's a lake just over there with an island in the middle, and I saw someone burying something.'

Lumpy Lawson put some sausages on the barbecue. He frowned deeply. 'How are we going to get to the island?' he asked. 'Islands are surrounded by water. I don't like water.'

'None of us likes water,' Captain Blackpatch pointed out. 'But if we want the treasure we are going to have to get across to that island somehow. I want you both to keep an eye out for some way of getting to the island, OK?'

Bald Ben and Lumpy both nodded. Lumpy turned the sausages over and dropped three of them into the long grass. He tried picking them up but they were rather hot. 'Yakky-yoo! Ow! Ow!' He dropped the sausages back in the grass, speared them angrily with a fork and popped them back on the barbecue, covered with wisps of dry grass.

'They look nice,' observed the Captain tartly.

'Herbs,' muttered Lumpy, sucking his burnt fingers. 'They're sprinkled with herbs. Campers always eat their sausages like this.'

'I think I'll have mine without, thank you all the same,' growled the Captain.

There was a loud noise in the distance, and a moment later Polly and Molly appeared, still running. They flung themselves into the depths of the tent, and even before they could start quarrelling Blackpatch was looming over them with a menacing scowl. 'Don't say a word,' he hissed, 'or you won't get any supper, and it's sausages – special sausages with herbs.'

Luckily, the twins were too puffed out to argue with Blackpatch, themselves or anyone at all. Hardly had the twins settled down than the boy with the binoculars went strolling past, took one look at Blackpatch, and ran straight to his mother in the tent next door.

'Mum! Mum! That man tried to take my binoculars *an'* he said he'd make me into sausages an' he said he's not scared of wimpy-pimpy women.'

Jack's mother came striding out of her tent, her jaw set and fire flashing in her eyes. She went straight up to Blackpatch and stabbed him in the chest with a dagger-like finger. 'Who are you . . .' **poke!** '. . . calling a wimpy-pimpy woman?' **poke!** 'You listen to me . . .' **poke! poke!** 'If you hurt my son . . .' **poke!** '. . . I'll pull that

137

silly hat down your head so far . . .' **poke!** '. . . that you'll be wearing it round your bony bottom like a skirt!' **poke!** 'Then we'll see who the wimpy-pimpy woman is!'

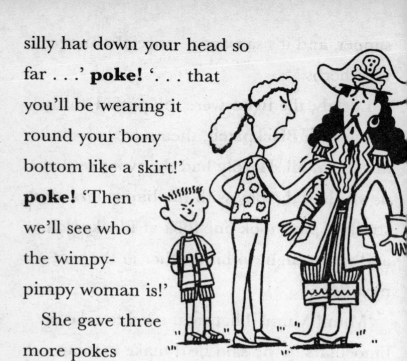

She gave three more pokes and Captain Blackpatch disappeared backwards into the back of the tent with a resounding crash. Jack's mother turned and stormed back to her own tent.

Bald Ben peered in at the Captain, who was lying in a crumpled heap on the floor.

'That was the lady who put up our tent,' he said. 'I told you she was nice.'

'She's not nice!' bellowed Blackpatch. 'And she's not a lady! She's a monster, a . . .

a dinosaur, a demon, a
dragon!'

Bald Ben stood
over the Captain
with his big arm
muscles twitching
angrily. He shook his
little bunch of flowers
at Blackpatch.
'Don't you call
her names,' he said.
'She put our tent up for us and that was
very nice of her, and I like her and I picked
these flowers for her!'

Captain Blackpatch groaned and sat up.
'Ben – you're a pirate! Pirates don't go
round the place giving wimpy women
bunches of flowers!'

'She can't have been that wimpy,' Bald
Ben baldly pointed out. 'She sorted you out,
didn't she?'

'I didn't want to hurt her,' snapped
Blackpatch. 'Anyhow, we must keep an eye
on her and that pesky Jack. He was with me
when I saw the island and I think he spotted
the treasure being buried too. I bet he's
after it.'

Even Bald Ben realized that this might
cause major trouble, and he stuck the
flowers in a plastic mug, put them on the
camping table and stared at them wistfully.
Lumpy Lawson finished the barbecue and
served up lumpy sausages to everyone,
including the Captain. (Lumpy had dropped
them again and now they had little clods of
mud clinging to them, as well as grass.)

That night, the pirates lay rocking in their
hammocks and whispering secret plans to
each other. 'Tomorrow we must think of a
way to reach the island,' muttered the
Captain.

'We could build a raft,' suggested Polly.

'I've got a better idea,' Molly hissed, but Blackpatch smacked his lips crossly and pulled a long wisp of grass from between his teeth. 'Nice sausages, Lumpy,' he murmured, before turning over and falling into a deep, treasure-full sleep.

4 On the Treasure Trail

Lumpy Lawson reckoned his brain would burst from the top of his head if he thought any harder. Even the twins were looking vaguely pensive. It was breakfast time and the pirates were sitting round the camping table and trying to think of a good way to reach the island.

'What about a bridge?' suggested Bald Ben.

'Too difficult,' chorused the others.

'A submarine . . .' Lumpy offered, and was met with looks of speechless horror from the others. The mere thought of being right *under* the water was too much to bear.

'A raft,' said Polly. 'I said last night we should make a raft.'

'It was my idea first,' Molly claimed.

'It was *not*! It was my idea, and I said it,

and everybody heard me.'

'Yeah, but I *thought* of it before you; I just didn't say anything.'

'Well, it doesn't count if you don't *say*,' Polly shouted indignantly.

'Does!'

'Doesn't!'

With one accord, the other three pirates drew their swords and threatened the twins with instant death if they didn't shut up. Captain Blackpatch tugged thoughtfully at his pointy chin. 'We've got to get that treasure. We shall have to find some kind of boat.'

'But, Captain, you always get seasick,'
Lumpy said gloomily.

'Surely you can't get seasick on a lake?'
Ben wanted to know. 'I've never heard of
anyone getting lake-sick. Anyhow, I've not
seen any boats around here.'

Blackpatch impatiently drummed his
fingers on the table. 'Neither have I. Maybe
we shall be able to find one in the town.'
This met with general approval so they
clambered into, or on to, the truck and off
they went to Bumpton, with the pirates
bouncing about in the back very
uncomfortably, all except for Captain
Blackpatch who sat in the front and drove
and felt very comfortable, thank you very
much.

Bumpton was a holiday town. It was full
of knick-knack shops and flags and balloons
and noisy people. Blackpatch was looking
for somewhere to park, but the only spot he

could find was marked 'DISABLED DRIVERS ONLY'. Blackpatch screeched to a halt. He jumped out of the truck, pulled one arm from his jacket-sleeve and hid his arm inside his jacket so that the sleeve looked empty.

'That's cheating,' scolded Bald Ben. Blackpatch rolled his eyes in despair.

'Ben, however did you become a pirate? Pirates are supposed to cheat . . . and rob, and steal, and generally be nasty.'

'Well, I don't think that's very nice,' Ben muttered moodily, and he trailed after the others as they followed their captain up the High Street.

Bumpton was not the best place to go for a boat hunt. The pirates searched and searched without success, until at last

Lumpy Lawson spotted something bright
and boat-ish hanging in the window of a
toyshop.

'Look, Captain! That's what we need.'
And there it was – a bright yellow, inflatable
dinghy. Blackpatch eyed it thoughtfully, and
wondered how they could steal it.

'Lumpy, you go inside and keep the shop-
keeper busy. When the right moment
comes, we'll nip in and
pinch the boat. Go
on, do your stuff!'
Lumpy was pushed
into the shop and
the shop-keeper
came forward to the
counter with a smile.
Lumpy's heart was in
his mouth. What *was* he to do?

'Can I help you?' asked the shop-keeper.

'Oh, um, yes, oh – look!' Lumpy suddenly

pointed up behind the shop-keeper's head. 'There's a butterfly.' The shop-keeper turned and gazed up behind him for a moment. Lumpy beckoned frantically to the others who were still waiting outside, but Blackpatch just made faces back at him.

'Go on!' mouthed the Captain crossly.

'I can't see a butterfly,' said the shop-keeper, quite mystified. Lumpy tried again.

'Oh, look – there's a gorilla in a bikini!'

The shop-keeper turned and looked where Lumpy was pointing, but Blackpatch's sword had stuck in his belt and he was having an almighty struggle. Lumpy was beginning to panic.

'Oh, look!' he said for the third time. 'There's a piano on fire and I think you ought to put it out.'

The shop-keeper gazed steadily at Lumpy. 'I'm sorry, sir, but I don't understand what kind of game you're playing. Now, is there anything you want?' Lumpy gave up in despair.

'Yes,' he sighed. 'We'd like that yellow boat and my friend out there in the big hat will pay for it.' Blackpatch marched inside, cursing Lumpy.

'Oh, well done,' he hissed, and he handed over some money to the shop-keeper.

'It's not my fault,' whispered Lumpy. 'You should have come in the first time.'

The Captain was a bit confused when he was handed a small cardboard box by the shop-keeper.

'What's this?' he demanded suspiciously.

'It's your dinghy,' the shop-keeper replied.

'No it isn't. Mine is much, much bigger than this.'

'Yes, sir, but this one doesn't have any air in it yet. When you get it home you take it

out of the box and pump it up.'

Luckily, Ben had seen an inflatable dinghy before and managed to convince the Captain that the shop-keeper wasn't trying to trick him. 'Not everyone cheats,' said Bald Ben, rather self-righteously, as they left the shop.

On the way back to the truck, the pirates bought some spades so that they could dig up the treasure. (Blackpatch was not going to risk another useless robbery.) They could almost feel the treasure jingling in their pockets, and their spirits rose.

As soon as they got back to the campsite, the Indoor Pirates began to put their plan into action. Blackpatch set Molly and Polly blowing up the dinghy by mouth, which was very cunning of him because it meant they couldn't quarrel with each other. Lumpy Lawson lay in his hammock recovering from his dreadful ordeal in the toyshop, while

Bald Ben hung about next door's tent with a silly grin on his face.

'Hello,' he said, when he caught sight of Jack and his mum.

'Hello,' said Jack's mum. 'You look busy next door. What are you doing?'

'Us? Oh, we're going trea . . . I mean, no we're not,' he added hastily. 'We're not at all.'

'Not what?' asked Jack's mum.

'I bet you're going to that island to dig for treasure,' said Jack, turning to his mum. 'Can I go too?'

'I don't think so, Jack,' said his mum. 'You shouldn't be playing with pirates. They're not nice.'

Bald Ben was stung. He hated it when

people didn't think he was nice. 'I'm all right,' he insisted. 'Really. I kissed a baby once.'

Jack's mum laughed quietly. 'You're all right, Ben,' she admitted. 'It's that other one I don't like – Blackpatch.' Ben shuffled his feet.

'The Captain's not bad really. He likes to behave as if he's bad.'

'I noticed,' said Jack's mum coldly. A sudden thought occurred to Ben.

'Don't go away,' he cried and he raced back to the pirate-tent, grabbed the plastic mug with its little bunch of flowers and went panting back next door. He handed the mug to Jack's mum. 'These are for you,' he said.

'Ben! Thank you – you are sweet!' Jack's mum leaned forward on tiptoe and kissed him on the cheek. Ben grinned so hard his face almost split in half. Jack stared at them both, stuck two fingers in his mouth and said he was going to be sick.

Blackpatch began yelling for everyone. The dinghy was all blown up and everything was ready.

'Come on,' he cried, and strode off towards the lake, leaving the others to carry the spades and the oars and the dinghy. It was only when they reached the shore of the lake that they realized the dinghy was too small to carry all of them. 'Someone will have to stay behind,' said the Captain.

'I know,' cried Molly, 'we can do "eeny-meeny-miny-mo" and the last one out can't go and it will be Polly.'

'No!' Polly shouted. 'We won't do "eeny-meeny", we'll do "ip-dip-dip, my little ship", and Molly gets left behind.'

While the twins were busy shouting, the others loaded the spades into the dinghy and set off. They were already a little way from the shore when the sisters realized what had happened. 'That's not fair!' they both cried, and for once they were in agreement, but there was nothing they could do about it.

'You two can't swim,' Blackpatch pointed out, then suddenly turned green and put his head over the side. Bald Ben steadied the little boat.

'Oh dear, maybe you can get lake-sick after all. Be careful, Captain, don't lean too far over. Your weight is pulling down the side of the dinghy and water's getting in.'

The warning was too late. Water was already pouring into the dinghy, turning the bottom into a miniature paddling pool, and the more the pirates struggled, the more water came sloshing over the sides.

'Bumblepoo!' yelled Lumpy Lawson. 'I've got a soggy botty!'

Captain Blackpatch tried to stand. He waved frantically back at Molly and Polly. 'Save us!' he shouted. 'We're drowning!' The twins stared at each other. Emergency! But where was the nearest help?

'You go that way,' cried Polly. 'I'll go this way.'

'No! You go this way and I'll
go that way!'

They set off, turned
about, crashed into each
other, set off again,
turned round, crashed
for a second time, got
up, hit each other, crashed
down, stood up, turned round, had another
crash and ended up sprawling in the sand
and trying to sit on each other's head.

Meanwhile, Blackpatch had fallen out of
the dinghy with a loud SPLOSH! and found
that the lake only came up to
his knees. 'I'm not
drowning!' he panicked,
before realizing it was
quite all right if he wasn't.
He struggled to his
feet. 'Hey, lads! It's all right – we're safe. We
can paddle back to shore. Come on.'

155

Bald Ben and Lumpy struggled out of the dinghy, which now had a puncture and no longer looked like a boat at all, but more like a large and useless popped balloon. Ben tucked the spades under his arm and they waded back to the shore.

'Thank you for rescuing us,' Blackpatch told the twins icily, and he squelched up the beach and back to the tent. He went inside, did up the zip, changed his clothes and went to bed, while Ben and Lumpy stood outside shivering, without even a towel between them.

'Can we come in?' asked Ben.

'No. I'm ill. Go away,' snarled the Captain.

Jack appeared next to Ben and he tugged at the pirate's wet trousers. 'Mum says you can change in her tent and dry off and she promises she won't look.' So Ben and Lumpy went next door to change. Jack's mum only had some towels and frilly blouses for them to wear, but she did make them a nice cup of tea. She gave Jack and the twins a glass of cola each and she even made sure that the glasses were all *exactly* the same size.

'This is wonderful,' sighed Ben, giving Jack's mum a big smile. She winked at him and he almost fell off his camping chair.

'You've gone very red, Ben,' Lumpy said.

'Sunburn,' muttered Ben, and hid his

 face behind his mug

of tea.

5 Blackpatch Has a Plan

'That dinghy was a fat lot of use,' grumbled Captain Blackpatch the next day.

'It was OK until you leaned over the side,' said Lumpy.

'Do you know what would have happened if I hadn't? I would have –'

'Maybe we can find another boat,' Bald Ben quickly suggested, and the Captain agreed.

'It's the only way we shall be able to get to that treasure. There must be a boat somewhere because I saw people on that island, and the only way they could have got there was if they had a boat.'

'They might have flown,' said Molly.

'Or floated down on a parachute,' said Polly.

'Or jumped,' Molly put in. Polly wrinkled her nose.

'Jumped? Don't be stupid. Nobody could jump that far.'

'Well then,' Molly sneered, 'if Nobody can jump that far perhaps it was Nobody who was on the island.'

'I'VE GOT AN IDEA!' roared Blackpatch, with his face fixed in his fiercest frown ever. 'Why don't we tie the twins up and leave them here while we go boat hunting in peace?'

'That's a good idea,' said Ben.

'That *is* a good idea!' agreed Lumpy, and they grabbed the girls, tied them back to back, and left them sitting by the tent looking thunderous from head to toe. Blackpatch gave them a parting smile.

'You see what can be done when people agree with each other instead of quarrelling! See you later, twins.'

The Indoor Pirates wandered down to the lake and once again found themselves staring wistfully across to the little island. The wood on the hill looked dark and green and secretive.

'I bet there's heaps of treasure buried over there,' Blackpatch said dreamily.

'Heaps . . .' murmured Lumpy, who was almost in a trance.

Bald Ben tugged at the Captain's sleeve. 'What's that thing on the water over there?' He pointed just round the corner of the lake near the campsite. 'It's not a swan, is it?'

'No, it isn't,' agreed the Captain, 'unless it's a swan with two heads. I think we had better investigate. Keep quiet, and crouch down in case someone sees.'

The three pirates crept round the edge of

the lake. The closer they got to the strange
thing the more astonished they became. A
peculiar noise drifted across the water . . .
schukka-schikka-squeak-schikka, schukka-
schikka-squeak-schikka.

'Shivering shrimps! It's a . . . boaty-
thingy-whatsit!' cried Blackpatch, and it was
too. On board the boaty-thingy-whatsit
were Jack and his mum. They were sitting
down and pedalling hard. What a strange
machine!

Jack's mum saw the pirates crouching by

the shore and called out to them from the pedalo she was riding. 'Hello, Ben!'

Ben was about to wave back cheerfully when Blackpatch seized him by the shoulder and pulled him down into the long grass. 'Get down!' he hissed. 'Before she spots you.'

'She already has spotted me. She only said "hello", and I was only going to say "hello" back.'

'Don't be stupid. She could be spying on us.'

Jack stood on his seat. 'Why are you all hiding in the grass?' he asked. 'Have you got a secret or something?' This was too much for Blackpatch, and he leaped up.

'We're not hiding,' he declared.

'You were,' said Jack. 'You were crouching in the grass.'

'No we weren't,' shouted Blackpatch. 'We fell over, that's what.' Jack's mum laughed.

'All of you – at the same time?'

'They didn't fall, Mum,' Jack insisted. 'They were hiding.'

'Why is that child so clever?' Blackpatch hissed under his breath. 'Nobody should be as clever as that. It's not natural.' He called out to the pair and asked them what their boaty-thing was.

'It's a pedalo,' said Jack, and he explained how it worked.

Blackpatch studied the small craft carefully. It was rather small and wobbly and it looked as if you could fall out all too easily. The Captain's stomach went queasy at the thought of taking to the water again so soon after his last little escapade.

However, there didn't seem to be any other choice, and gradually a cunning smile slid across beneath his pointy nose.

Blackpatch pulled the other two further along the beach until they could see the tiny pedalo harbour. There they counted ten pedalos altogether. Some were out on the lake and others were roped to a little jetty. Two men were standing on the jetty, taking people's money and showing them to their pedalos.

Captain Blackpatch's eyes narrowed to sneaky slits. 'We are going to be rich, lads,' he whispered. 'We are going to be very rich and it is all going to happen tonight.'

'Tonight?' repeated Lumpy. 'Have you got a plan, Captain?' Blackpatch nodded.

'We come down here tonight, on tiptoe,

very, very quietly, when everyone is
asleep . . .'

'Will we be asleep?' asked Ben, who liked
a good night's snooze.

'Of course not! We shall be out here,
doing a bit of skulduggery.'

'What's skulduggery?' Ben asked, hoping
that it didn't mean having to be nasty to
anyone.

'Skulduggery is what pirates do at night,'
explained Blackpatch. 'Stop asking awkward
questions. Listen, we come down here
tonight and we steal some pedalos. Then we
nip across to the island and dig up the
treasure and come back here and . . .'
Blackpatch broke off and beamed knowingly
at the others.

'Go to sleep?' Ben finished hopefully.

'No! We'll have the treasure, won't we?
We shall be rich! We run away with the
treasure and live happily ever after.'

'And *then* we go to sleep,' Ben added with
a smile.

'Yes, Ben, after that you can sleep for a
thousand years if you want, in a bed as big
as a bandstand and as soft as duck-down.'

'Wow!' breathed Ben rapturously.

'Come on,' urged the Captain. 'We must
get back to the twins and tell them what the
plan is.'

Back on the campsite, there was a bit of
a commotion going on. Jack and his mum
had finished their pedalo ride and gone
back to their tent, only to discover that
Polly and Molly were rolling about tied
back to back. They were covered in dirt
and grass and furiously kicking their legs
in the air.

'Those poor pirate children,' said Jack's
mum. 'How on earth did they get in that
state?'

'The Captain tied us up!' cried Polly.

'Yeah, an' Lumpy and Ben!' shouted
Molly.

'That's dreadful,' said Jack's mum, hastily
untying them. 'You poor things. Jack, get
Molly and Polly a drink. Those pirates
aren't fit to look after themselves, let alone
two children.'

Molly and Polly slurped down their drinks
in no time at all and then played with Jack.
He proudly showed them his paddling toy.
It was an enormous green inflatable
crocodile, with handles down the back that

you could hold on to while you sat on it and paddled. 'My gran gave it to me,' Jack said.

'It's enormous,' said Polly.

'It's huge,' said Molly.

'That's just what I said,' Polly pointed out.

'No – you said "enormous" and I said "huge".'

'Yeah? They mean the same thing –'

'No they don't. Huge is bigger than enormous.'

'It is *not*! Enormous is much bigger than huge. Enormous is as big as, as big as . . . the whole universe!' cried Polly. Molly folded her arms in triumph.

'In that case, this crocodile can't be enormous, or it would be as big as the universe and it wouldn't even fit in this tent,' she declared. 'And that means it's huge – like I said.'

'Girls!' laughed Jack's mum. 'It doesn't

matter how big it is. If you ask Jack nicely I'm sure he'll let you have a go on it tomorrow.' Her soft face suddenly became tense. 'The other pirates are coming back. Good – I want a word with them.'

What took place after that wasn't very nice – at least it certainly was not very nice for Ben and Lumpy and Blackpatch. Jack's mum was furious at the way they had left the twins all tied up, and she made it quite clear that she thought they were monsters. Blackpatch carefully stood behind Ben and Lumpy so that if this dreadful woman started poking with her finger again they would get the worst of it.

But Bald Ben didn't care how much he got poked. He was overcome with despair when he discovered that the nice lady from next door was so cross with him. He gazed at her with huge puppy-dog eyes. He felt as if his whole world had collapsed and he didn't care how rich he was going to be.

Molly and Polly came out of Jack's tent and sauntered cockily past the stunned pirates. 'She told you!' hissed Molly with immense satisfaction.

'Yeah,' agreed Polly, and the two sisters turned to each other and slapped their hands together like a pair of jubilant

footballers. The other pirates gawked at each other. Did they really see what they had just seen? Incredible!

6 Treasure Island at Last

In the dead of night, the Indoor Pirates crept out of their tent. 'Are you ready?' hissed Captain Blackpatch. 'Are you all on tiptoe?'

'Yes, Cap'n.'

'Good – follow me.' He turned to go and almost leaped out of his skin as he came face to face with a huge green monster.

'Aaargh!' Blackpatch was trembling in his boots. He clung to Bald Ben like a scared monkey and pointed at the green beast with its snapping jaws and great white fangs.

'It's only Jack's inflatable crocodile,' said Lumpy. 'He goes paddling on it.'

Blackpatch glared at the toy perched against Jack's tent. 'That child will be the death of me,' he muttered, then set off once more, creeping past the other tents. This time they reached the lake without further incident and quietly crept on to the jetty. The pedalos were still and silent, floating on the dark waters of the lake. Blackpatch climbed on a pedalo, sat down and hunted for the rope that tied it to the jetty, only to discover to his horror that it wasn't tied with a rope any longer.

A heavy chain fastened the pedalo to a stake, and the heavy chain had an even heavier padlock clamped through the links.

'They're all locked up!' he cried. 'Stupid, stupid people! Why have they chained them up?'

'I suppose they don't want anyone to steal them,' said Bald Ben, who thought it was a very sensible thing to do.

Blackpatch swiped his hat from his head and began battering Ben with it.

'You cod-brained bladder-wrack! Of course they don't want anyone to steal them, but we've got to get to Treasure Island, and now we can't.'

Polly and Molly had got an idea, and it was quite a good one. 'Why don't we use Jack's crocodile?' said Molly, and her sister nodded. 'It's probably big enough for all of us, and we can use the spades as paddles.'

Blackpatch allowed this neat idea to roll about his brain for a few moments. What a wonderful way to get even with that smart little clever-clogs from the tent next door – they could use his favourite toy to grab the treasure! 'Right, lads – back to the campsite – everyone on tiptoe again.'

Off they went, creeping back to Jack's tent where the green beast was still standing on its tail and looking menacing by moonlight. Lumpy took the front end of the crocodile and Blackpatch took the tail because, even though it was made of plastic, the Captain didn't like to get right next to those sharp teeth. A little voice came from the tent. 'Who's that out there?' Jack asked sleepily.

'Nobody,' hissed Blackpatch. 'Go back to sleep or I'll chop your ears off.' This met with silence so the pirates set off for the lake. On the way there they had a stroke of luck because Bald Ben spotted an inflatable duck outside another tent.

174

'That will do me nicely,' he told the others. 'I don't like crocodiles – too many teeth.'

Back at the campsite, Jack lay in his bed dreamily thinking to himself. There must have been somebody outside  because they had spoken to him. He sat up with a jerk. He had just remembered what they'd said. They'd threatened to chop his ears off. That wasn't very nice! Jack leaned out of bed and shook his mother.

'Mum? Mum? Someone is outside and they said that if I didn't go to sleep they'd cut off my ears.'

This was quite enough to put Jack's mum on red-alert and she rose from her bed like an Amazon warrior and threw herself outside with an angry yell. 'Who wants to chop off my son's ears?' she demanded, and was surprised to find nobody there.

This changed quickly, because the occupants of all the tents near by were roused by her shout and campers came crawling out in their pyjamas and nightgowns demanding to know what was going on, and waving torches in all directions.

'Somebody has been prowling around,' said Jack's mum accusingly. Jack came outside, took one look and burst into tears.

'My crocodile's been stolen!' he wailed.

Jack's mum strode across to the pirates'

tent and poked her head inside. 'Just as I thought. There's nobody here. The pirates must have stolen Jack's crocodile.'

'My spotty duck's gone too,' cried an elderly lady. 'Come on, they must have taken them to the lake. Let's get after them!' With a cry of 'Get the pesky pirates!' the campers hurried off to the lake.

The Indoor Pirates were doing quite well. Blackpatch, Lumpy and Polly were sitting on the giant crocodile, merrily paddling away. The Captain was so excited at the thought of all the treasure that he quite

forgot to worry about being seasick, or lake-sick, or any kind of sick. Molly and Ben were on the duck, and they all found that the spades made excellent paddles. It did not take them long to reach the island. The pirates leaped ashore and scrambled up the beach.

'Treasure Island!' cried Blackpatch. 'At last!'

'Treasure Island!' echoed the others. 'Where do we dig, Cap'n?'

Captain Blackpatch studied the beach carefully. 'I reckon it must have been about here.' He prodded the sand with his spade. 'Get digging!'

The pirates set to with gusto, each digging in a different place. Sand was flying in every direction and soon Molly and Polly were back to their usual antics. 'Every time you take sand out of your hole you throw it into mine,' Polly complained.

'I'm only giving you your sand back,' said
Molly, 'because you took it from your hole
and put it in mine first of all.'

'Just dig,' bellowed Blackpatch. 'We're
here to find treasure, not to argue.'

The pirates dug and dug. They dug here
and they dug there, without finding so much
as a pebble. They were almost ready to give
up when Lumpy's spade struck something
hard. 'I've found it, Captain!' he cried.
'There's a lump down here!'

The Indoor Pirates gathered round
Lumpy's pit and watched with round eyes as
he pushed his spade deep into the sand and
began to lever out something large. The

sand heaved and broke and trickled off the spade leaving the treasure in full view of everyone.

'It's . . .' began Blackpatch. 'It's . . .' He couldn't believe his eyes.

'It's rubbish,' muttered Bald Ben. 'Someone has been here and they've had a barbecue and a picnic and they've buried all their rubbish.'

The five pirates stared into the hole at their broken dreams. At the bottom of the pit lay a pile of burnt charcoal, several scraggy meat bones, some very sandy sandwiches (half-eaten) and some rotting bits of tomato and lettuce.

'I thought you said they'd buried treasure,' Lumpy accused the Captain.

'How was I to know they were burying rubbish?' cried Blackpatch angrily. 'I mean, what a stupid, stupid, STUPID thing to bury! Why would anyone bury rubbish?!'

'So it doesn't make a mess, of course,' Bald Ben said.

A shout drifted across the water from the distant shore. 'There they are, on the island! After them!' The campers poured on to the jetty. Someone produced a key and the pedalos were unchained. Brandishing their torches like clubs, the campers began pedalling across the lake at full speed, with Jack and his mum in the lead and foam spurting from the churning paddles.

Captain Blackpatch turned white. 'Don't let that horrible pokey woman anywhere near me!' he cried, and he leaped on to Jack's crocodile. Lumpy and Polly joined him and they desperately tried to escape the fast-approaching armada of pedalos. Ben and Molly were close behind on their giant spotted duck, paddling furiously.

'Faster, faster!' cried Blackpatch, his spade flashing in the water, and he gripped the crocodile with his legs to stop himself slipping off.

Unfortunately, he squeezed the inflatable toy so hard that the crocodile could no longer contain itself. The bung suddenly shot from its tail and a jet of air screeched out, sending the crocodile skimming across the water with the pirates hanging on for dear life. 'Help!' yelled Blackpatch, as the jet-propelled croc went whizzing backwards and forwards and round and round like a crazy balloon. Up and down it went, with the air rushing from its tail –
SPLURRRRRRRRRR!!!

At last it ran out of wind, went completely floppy and left the pirates floundering in the water. Blackpatch discovered that this time the lake didn't come up to his knees but well above his hat.

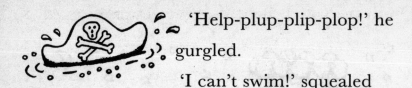 'Help-plup-plip-plop!' he gurgled.

'I can't swim!' squealed Polly, and she couldn't.

'I'll save you!' Molly shouted.

'But you can't swim either!' spluttered Polly, vanishing beneath the surface.

'Yes I can!' cried Molly and bravely dived in, sank and reappeared briefly. 'No I can't!' she agreed and sank again.

There was a loud splash as Jack's mum threw herself from her pedalo and dived into the black water. A moment later she reappeared with both twins, who immediately spurted fountains of water from their mouths, along with one or two startled fish. As the pedalos reached the pirates, other hands grabbed Blackpatch and Lumpy and pulled them

from the water. Bald Ben gave himself up
and was towed back to the shore.

Everyone was rather wet and cross. Jack's
mum confronted a very bedraggled Captain
Blackpatch. 'You'd cut off my son's ears,
would you?' **Poke!** 'We'll see about that!'
Poke! She reached up, grabbed the
Captain's ears and
gave them a good pull.

'Yow!' he cried.

Jack smiled and
looked up at the pirate

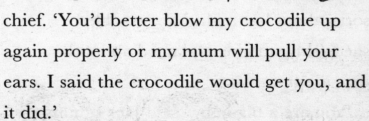

chief. 'You'd better blow my crocodile up
again properly or my mum will pull your
ears. I said the crocodile would get you, and
it did.'

'It's your mum that's the crocodile,' hissed
Blackpatch and everyone burst out laughing.

The campers went back to bed, and so
did the pirates, all except for Blackpatch.
He was left on his own, huffing and puffing

all night long. By the time morning came, the crocodile was fully inflated and Blackpatch was lying next to it, fully deflated and snoring his hat off.

Bald Ben went to next door's tent. 'I'm sorry about last night,' he mumbled sheepishly, and he explained about the treasure hunt.

'You are a big baby,' said Jack's mum. 'Fancy wanting to play with a plastic crocodile. However did you get to be a pirate?'

'My mum was a pirate and my dad was a pirate. They taught me everything I know.'

'It wasn't much, was it?' laughed Jack's mum. Jack grabbed Ben by the hand.

'When I grow up I'm going to be a pirate,' he said, and his mother sighed.

'See what you've started?' But she gave Ben a bright smile and he came over all funny and turned red from head to toe. He went back to the pirate tent feeling a great deal happier.

Captain Blackpatch had woken up and was

now slumped back against Jack's crocodile. 'This holiday has been terrible,' he complained. 'There's been no treasure at all. Maybe it's time we went home.' But the other pirates didn't feel like going home. They were just getting used to camping. Lumpy had even stopped dropping the sausages in the grass.

'Can't we stay a bit longer?' they pleaded. Blackpatch gazed moodily back at them.

At that moment, Jack came across from his tent. He had his binoculars round his neck. He had a wooden sword stuck in his belt and a red spotted scarf tied on his head. 'I'm a pirate,' he declared, 'and I'm going on a treasure hunt. Who's coming with me?'

'Me!' cried Lumpy and Ben and the twins, and they set off at once. Blackpatch watched them for a few seconds.

'Wait for me!' he yelled and hurried after them.

Jeremy Strong

Giant Jim and the Hurricane

Illustrated by Nick Sharratt

For Poppy

Contents

1 How to Arrest a Giant

There was a very strange noise coming from beyond the window. Constable Dunstable sat up in bed and scratched his head. It was half-past six in the morning. What could be making such a noise? He got out of bed, went across to the window and pulled back the curtains.

'Aargh!' Constable Dunstable leaped
back. Staring through the window at him
was a huge face, with a ginger beard as
big as a forest and –

the face belonged to a head, and
the head belonged to a body, and
the body had two long, hairy arms,
and two huge legs.

'It's a giant!' cried Constable Dunstable. He ran downstairs and ran across the room. He opened his front door and ran outside, right between the giant's legs, and he carried on running and running, still in his pyjamas.

'There's a giant in our town!' yelled Constable Dunstable as he hurried through the streets.

Windows were thrown open. Sleepy people poked out their heads to see what all the fuss was about.

'Well I never!' murmured Mrs Sniffling. 'Constable Dunstable is running round the streets in his pyjamas. He is shouting something about a giant.'

'A giant?' sniffed Mr Sniffling, and he sat up in bed. 'I don't believe in giants.'

'I think you might believe in this one,' said his wife. 'Because this giant is

standing at the end of our road. He is as
tall as four houses sitting on top of each
other, and he is holding a giant saucepan
in one hand and a giant wicker basket in
the other, and he has a giant saxophone
strapped to his back.'

Mr Sniffling growled and climbed out
of his nice, warm bed. He went to the
window. 'Oh!' he cried. 'A giant! There's
a giant in our town!'

'Do you know, that is exactly what
Constable Dunstable was saying,' said
Mrs Sniffling. 'Look, now *you* are
running round in your pyjamas too!'

It was quite true. Mr Sniffling was racing down the street in his pyjamas. In fact, almost half the town were rushing about in pyjamas and nightdresses, and they were all shouting at each other.

'A giant! A giant! We shall all be squashed!' cried Mr Sniffling.

'We shall all be squished!' squeaked Mrs Goodbody. She hurried across to

Constable Dunstable. 'Arrest that giant at once!' she insisted.

Constable Dunstable looked up at the giant's big, ginger head and swallowed hard. He was an awfully big person to arrest.

'I shall have to put my uniform on and get my handcuffs and my *Giant-Spotter's Handbook*. Then you can all come with

me and we will arrest the giant and shoo him out of our town. We don't want giants here.'

'No! We don't want giants in our town!' everyone shouted.

'What's wrong with giants?' asked little Poppy Palmer, the farmer's daughter. But nobody listened. She thought the giant looked rather nice.

The crowd marched off behind Constable Dunstable and waited patiently until the policeman had changed into his uniform. When Constable Dunstable came back out they all got up and marched behind him once again, and that helped him feel a bit braver.

They went up the road and there was the giant, standing at the other end and frowning down at them with his great big, bearded face. The crowd stopped.

Mr Sniffling pushed Constable Dunstable forward.

'Go on,' he muttered. 'Arrest that giant at once.'

Constable Dunstable took two wobbly steps forward and then stopped. He pressed his knees together very hard, so that he couldn't hear them knocking any longer. He stared up and UP and UP.

'I arrest you in the name of the law!' he cried. 'Put on these handcuffs at once!'

The giant looked at the tiny handcuffs. They were much too small for his great hands. Carefully he put down his saucepan and his wicker basket and gently held out his hands. Constable Dunstable just managed to push the handcuffs over the tips of the giant's fingers. He snapped them shut.

'There,' said Constable Dunstable.
'Now you are our prisoner. I am going to
put you in jail for years and years and
years.'

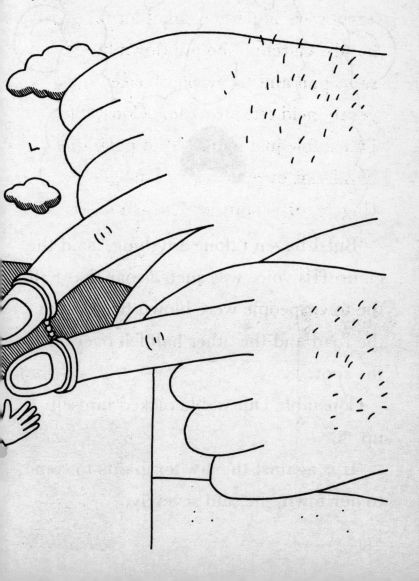

'But I haven't done anything,' said the giant. His voice was such a roar that half the townspeople were blown back down the road and the other half fell over on the spot.

Constable Dunstable picked himself up.

'It is against the law for giants to come to our town,' he said severely.

'That isn't very fair,' said the giant,
and everyone fell over again. Constable
Dunstable picked himself up.

'AND – you keep knocking everyone
over.'

'I can't help it,' said the giant, and
everyone fell over again. Constable
Dunstable picked himself up for the third
time.

'Then I shall have to put you in jail
for ever and ever!' said the policeman.

And that was when the giant began to cry. Huge tears filled his eyes, trickled down his cheeks and crashed to the ground far below.

'Stop it!' cried the soaking townspeople. 'We shall all drown!'

This made the giant cry even more, and it was just like two long, thin, sparkling waterfalls. The giant cried for half the morning. Soon there was a little pool of tears, and the pool became a pond, and the pond became a lake. Some people got out their umbrellas and some people got out their boats, but the children got out their swimming costumes and swam about splashing each other.

Mrs Careless, the Mayoress, was becoming most concerned. 'We can't have this,' she told Constable Dunstable.

'We must do something. This lake will start overflowing any minute and then the whole town will be flooded. Tell the giant you won't arrest him if he stops crying.'

So Constable Dunstable told the giant to stop crying.

'I won't arrest you,' he explained. 'But you must promise to be a good giant.'

'I am a good giant,' snivelled the giant, and he blew his nose –

SSPPPPLLLLLUUURRRRRGGGGHHH!

– and everyone who wasn't swimming
fell over, and half the rowing boats were
overturned, and Constable Dunstable
disappeared into the lake.

'I have always been a good giant,' the giant added, poking a helpful finger into the lake and hooking Constable Dunstable back on to dry land.

'Do you think you could speak more softly?' asked Mrs Goodbody. 'Every time you speak it makes a terrible wind and we all fall over. And please don't sneeze.'

'Sorry,' said the giant, and everyone fell over.

'Sorry,' he said again, very quietly, and everyone picked themselves up.

The policeman glared angrily at the giant.

'Right then, you sit down on that hill. You are going to have to answer some questions.'

'Oh good! Is it a quiz, like on television? Will I win a painting set?'

asked the giant, sitting himself down on the hill with an enormous, thunderous thump.

'Not exactly. First of all, question one: What is your name?'

'Jim.'

'I want your full name,' said the policeman.

'Oh. Giant Jim.'

'Question two: Where do you live?'

'That's obvious,' said Giant Jim with such a big smile that his whole beard went crinkly. 'I live right here.'

2 Homeless and Hopeless

'Here!' cried everyone else. 'In our town?'

'Well, I would like to live here,' said Giant Jim. 'It's nice here. You've got a lake and everything.'

'We didn't have a lake until you came here and started crying,' sniffed Mr Sniffling.

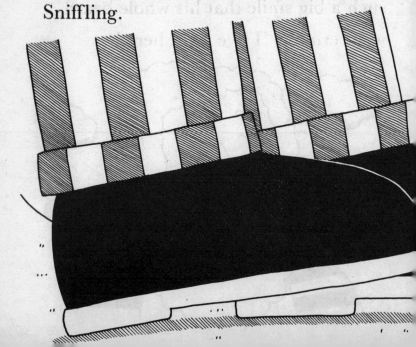

'But it *is* a nice lake,' said Poppy Palmer. 'We can go rowing and swimming and sail our boats.'

'You might fall in,' warned the children's mothers.

'We like falling in!' shouted the children.

'I am not at all sure about this,' said Constable Dunstable. 'Giants can be very dangerous. How do we know that you won't eat anyone?'

Giant Jim looked most hurt. 'Of course I won't eat anyone. I don't eat meat. I'm a vegetable.'

'I think you mean that you are a vegetarian,' said Poppy Palmer.

The giant grinned. 'That's right. I'm a vegenariable!'

'Well, I don't know,' grumbled Constable Dunstable, and he got out his *Giant-Spotter's Handbook*. He thumbed through the pages.

'Have you only got one eye? No? You're not a Cyclops then. Have you got a golden harp and a hen?'

'I don't have a golden harp, but I do have a hen!' cried the giant. 'You are clever! How did you know that? I have a hen in my wicker basket here,' and he tapped the big basket.

Constable Dunstable took several steps back.

'If you've got a hen then you could be a Beanstalk Giant. My book says that Beanstalk Giants are very, very dangerous. They eat humans.'

The giant looked heartbroken and he shook his head sadly. 'But I don't eat people. I eat vegetables and eggs. That's why I have my hen. Her name is Florence Fluffybum and she lays eggs for me. I put them in my saucepan and I have scrambled eggs, boiled eggs, or maybe an omelette or egg-bread . . .'

'Yes, yes, all right,' muttered the

policeman. 'You're not a Beanstalk Giant then. How about a Big Friendly Giant? Do you do dreams? Is that a dream-puffer strapped to your back?'

The giant shook his head.

'No, this is my saxophone.'

Constable Dunstable turned over the page and his face lit up.

'Ah! Now I've got you! If that's a saxophone then you must be a Jazz Giant!'

'A Jazz Giant,' murmured Giant Jim. 'I'm a Jazz Giant.'

'That's right. And my book says that Jazz Giants are harmless, cheerful, but often noisy, especially if they play the drums.'

'I don't play the drums. I play the saxophone,' said Jim with a big smile. He swung his saxophone across his front.

A moment later the air was shattered by an explosion of music and everybody fell over yet again.

The nearby trees had half their leaves blown off. The terrified sheep ran round their field so fast that the sheep at the front caught up with the sheep at the back and they all collided in a big heap. The cows tumbled on to their backs and waved their legs in the air, with their udders wobbling about like big, pink jellies.

'Stop! Stop!' yelled Constable Dunstable, with both hands clasped over his ears.

Giant Jim put down his saxophone.

'Did you like that?' he grinned. 'I'm a very good saxophone player.'

The townspeople struggled back to their feet, shaking their ringing heads. 'You *are* a very good saxophone player,' they agreed. 'But please don't play so loudly.'

'It was brilliant!' yelled the children, who always liked a free disco.

Constable Dunstable was rather relieved that Giant Jim did not play the drums. After all, if the giant saxophone knocked everybody off their feet, giant drums would probably start an earthquake. However, he still had some important questions to ask.

'Where are you going to live?' he
wanted to know.

The giant gazed down at Poppy
Palmer. 'I'd like to live with you,' he said.

'Oh!' said Poppy. 'That's nice, but our
house is too small for you.'

'It's a farmhouse,' grunted Mr Palmer
the farmer. 'It's for farmers.'

'Then I shall live with you!' said
Giant Jim, pointing at Constable
Dunstable.

'No, you can't,' said the policeman
firmly. 'I live in the Police House and
it's just for policemen.'

'In that case,' smiled Giant Jim, 'if the
Farmhouse is for farmers, and the Police
House is for policemen, I shall live in the
Giant House.'

Everyone looked at each other.

'The Giant House?' they muttered.

Wherever was the Giant House? Constable Dunstable frowned.

'We haven't got a Giant House, because giants have never lived here. You are homeless and you will have to sleep outside on the hills until you find a house for yourself. Now, be very careful where you tread because you are big and everything else round here is small and you don't fit in.'

With that, Constable Dunstable set off back to the town and everyone followed, except for Poppy Palmer and her best friend, Crasher. (He was called Crasher because he ran around so fast that he kept crashing into things. He also crashed *out* of things – like trees, when he was halfway up them.)

Giant Jim stared after the disappearing townspeople.

'I'm homeless,' he muttered.
'Everybody has a home except me. I'm
homeless and hopeless.'

'There's nothing wrong with you,' said
Crasher, trying to cheer up the giant.

'Oh yes there is. My feet are too big . . .'

'They *are* quite large,' agreed the
children.

'And my legs are too big . . .'

'They are a bit like tree trunks,'
nodded Crasher.

'And my chest is too big . . .'

'It is – huge!' murmured Poppy.

'And my head is too big.'

Poppy and Crasher looked at each
other. 'You are *very* big,' they said.

'But that doesn't mean that you are
hopeless,' said Poppy. 'I bet you can do
lots of things. You've already made us a
lake.'

'I didn't mean to,' said Giant Jim.

'I know, but it's a lovely lake. We've always wanted a lake, and so we are going to help you find a home.'

'Thank you,' said Giant Jim, and he looked a lot happier. A moment of silence passed and then he asked, 'Have you found one yet?'

'No!' Crasher laughed. 'It will probably take a little bit of time. Come on, Poppy, let's go house-hunting.' Crasher raced off, tripped over his own laces and went crashing all the way to the bottom of the hill.

Poppy ran after him, and the two children spent the rest of the morning searching for a Giant House, and the whole afternoon, and most of the evening too. They had no luck at all. At nine o'clock that night they had to tell Giant Jim that they hadn't found anywhere.

'You will have to stay out here tonight,' said Poppy. 'But I'm sure we will find somewhere for you tomorrow. Will you be all right?'

'Of course I shall,' smiled Giant Jim bravely. 'Giants are always all right. Goodnight.'

3 A Bed for the Night

Night-time came. The sky grew dark and the streets of the town were silent. People switched on their lights and turned on their televisions. Giant Jim sat on the hill and gazed down dreamily at the sleepy town.

Quiet, chirrupy noises came from inside his big wicker basket. 'Oh!' murmured Giant Jim. 'Florence Fluffybum! I forgot all about you. Come on, out you come.' Giant Jim opened the lid of the basket and out stepped Florence Fluffybum.

She had speckled, silvery-grey feathers,
eyes like sparkling glass,
a sticking-up tail,

and long, brown legs with
knibbly-knobbly knees,
and huge splayed toes,
and she was as big as a conker tree.

'Prrrrk,' said Florence Fluffybum,
pecking some food from the ground.
With a flutter of happy-flappy wings,
she jumped on to Giant Jim's head. He
reached up and stroked her soft grey
feathers.

'What are we going to do, Florrie?'
asked Giant Jim.

'Prrrrk,' answered the hen softly.

'Everyone has gone home to bed, and
we are left outside in the dark.'

'Prrrrk,' said Florrie.

'I wish we had a bed and a home.'

'Prrrrk,' said Florrie. The hen glanced
quickly all around. She jumped off Giant

Jim's head and stalked down to the edge
of the town. Florence Fluffybum looked
carefully at every building, which was
quite easy for her, because she was as big
as most of them. Florence Fluffybum
seemed to be looking for something, and
eventually she found it.

236

Florrie lifted her feet carefully, stepped through the town streets and stood outside the library. The library had a great big flat roof. It was just the right place for a giant hen to roost for the night.

'Prrrrrk,' sighed Florrie, climbing on to the roof. She settled her feathers, tucked her head in and closed her eyes.

Giant Jim sadly rubbed his big, ginger beard.

'It's all right for you,' he muttered. 'What about me? Where shall I sleep?'

One by one the night-time stars came out. Giant Jim lay down on the hillside and tried to sleep. He tossed and he turned. He could not make himself comfy at all. He tried counting Farmer Palmer's sheep. He picked them up one by one and put them in another field. 'One, two, three, four . . .'

By the time Giant Jim reached 137 there were no sheep left, so he began picking up the ducks from the river and putting them in the cow field. Then he counted all the cows by picking them up and putting them in the river, which came as a bit of a surprise to the cows, who didn't think it was bath-time at all. Luckily the river was not deep. The cows stood there watching the water swirl slowly round their big fat bellies and wondered why they felt wet.

Finally Giant Jim gave up trying to
sleep. He fetched his saxophone and
began playing himself a gentle lullaby.
At once windows began opening up and

down the town in every street. Angry
heads poked out and shouted at the
giant. 'Oi! Stop that horrible racket.
We're trying to sleep!' And the
townspeople threw their old boots at
him. They rained down upon the giant
and several boots went right inside his
saxophone, making it go all squeaky.

Giant Jim put down his instrument,
lay on his back and stared up at the
night sky.

'I don't think people like me very much,' he thought. 'They think I'm too big and noisy and clumsy. I can't help it. That's the way I am. If they were all big like me they wouldn't notice.'

He sighed heavily and gazed across the town. His eye caught something interesting and he sat up and looked more carefully.

'I spy a Giant House,' murmured Giant Jim happily, and sure enough there, right on the edge of the little town, stood the Dance Hall, and it was just the right size for a giant.

'All I have to do,' thought Jim, 'is take off the lid.'

He bent down, grasped the roof on both sides and pulled it off, just like taking the lid off a box. Then he lay down inside.

BUT –

– it was dark, and Giant Jim did not see all the chairs and tables, so they all got crushed.

Giant Jim lifted his head and noticed the big stage where the town band always played. 'That will make an excellent resting place for my head,' he sighed happily, and he laid his head upon the stage.

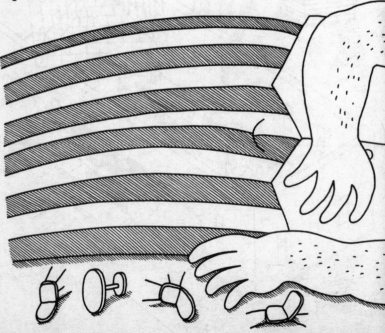

BUT –

– it was dark, and Giant Jim didn't see
all the band's instruments lying there, so
they all got squashed. There were:

squidged trumpets,
and squodged tubas,
and squoodged flutes,
squeezed oboes, squoozed clarinets,
and squozzlicated trombones.

And as for all the violins – they had been turned into matchsticks.

Giant Jim gave a loud snore, turned on to his side, flattened the drum-set and slept like a child. (A very, very, VERY BIG CHILD!)

4   Disasters Everywhere

Giant Jim slept so well that he did not wake up until he was disturbed by a strange roaring noise, and a splashy feeling all over his face. He opened his eyes, only to have a bucket of cold water tossed in his face by Mrs Careless, the Mayoress.

Behind the Mayoress stood an angry crowd of townspeople.

'Look what you've done!' they yelled. 'You've smashed our Dance Hall! You've smashed all our instruments. We are supposed to be having our Grand Disco Dance next week. Now what are we going to do?' And they all began to shout things at Giant Jim.

'You're the biggest, clumsiest oaf in the world!'

'You're the stupidest giant that ever was!'

'And your hen's laid an egg on our library!'

Giant Jim was even more upset than the townspeople. He muttered 'Sorry! I'm sorry!' over and over again. He stood up and tried to mend all the instruments, but he only made matters worse. He tried to put the Dance Hall roof back on, but it crumpled in his hands and all the tiles smashed round his feet, as if he'd just dropped a big bag of marbles.

'Go away!' cried Mrs Careless. 'You giant, ginger, jelly-brain!'

'Leave us in peace!' shouted Mr Sniffling. 'Giants always cause trouble wherever they go, and we don't want trouble here. I want to change my library book,' he complained, 'but I can't because your giant hen is laying eggs on top of the library. Has she got a card? If she hasn't got a library card she's not allowed in the library – or *on* the library,' he added sniffily. Mr Sniffling was backed up by a noisy crowd who shouted that hens weren't allowed in the library anyway.

'You'd better do something,' Poppy Palmer warned Giant Jim.

Giant Jim reached down and picked
up Florence Fluffybum, but he was in
such a fluster that he dropped her egg
and it fell –

KER-SPLATT!

– right on to the library roof, and
cracked open. Egg splattered out all over
the streets. It dribbled down the library
walls and windows.

'Urgh!' yelled Mrs Careless, the
Mayoress. 'I've got egg on my best frock.'

'Splurgh!' cried Mr Goodbody. 'I've
got egg on my head.'

Farmer Palmer came running up the
High Street. 'That stupid giant has put
all my sheep in the cornfield, and all my
ducks in the cow field, and all my cows
in the river!'

'Stupid, stupid giant!' yelled the crowd.

And then someone in the crowd threw an egg at Giant Jim.

It hit the giant on his knee. A jeer went up from the crowd, and a moment later everybody seemed to be throwing eggs at the poor giant and shouting at him and calling him names. He hurried away, clutching Florence Fluffybum, with eggs hitting his back and trickling down to his feet.

Poppy Palmer tried desperately to stop everyone. But nobody could hear her small voice above the cheering and jeering. Poppy stood in the town square, watching the yelling crowd chase after the giant, and tears rolled down her cheeks.

'How can they be so horrid?' she

cried. 'He only wants to be friends.'

Giant Jim stumbled stickily to the
edge of the lake. He couldn't bear to feel
all that egg and eggshell clinging to him.
He plunged into the lake with all his
clothes on and started washing
frantically. Water began to slop over the
edges of the lake.

It sploshed out over the top.
It splished out over the bottom,
and it splashed out all the way
down the edges.

A stream of water began to trickle
towards the town and the more Giant
Jim splashed around, trying to get rid of
all that egg, the more water went down
the hill. Soon the stream became a
brook, and the brook became a river,

and the river became a flood, and the
flood became a –

DISASTER!

'Help!' yelled Mrs Careless, the
Mayoress. 'We're all going to drown!
Now look what you've done!'

'There's a fish swimming round my
living room,' complained Mrs
Goodbody.

'There are frogs hopping up and down
my stairs,' squeaked Mr Sniffling.

Constable Dunstable got out his
bicycle and rode through the wet streets
waving his pair of handcuffs.

'Now I shall really have to arrest the
giant,' he said severely.

Poppy and Crasher were most upset.

'It's not the giant's fault,' they cried.

'He was only trying to get himself clean, and the only reason he was dirty was because you threw eggs at him.'

'Well, he threw an egg at us,' sniffed Mrs Sniffling, 'and it was a very big egg.'

'He didn't throw it. He dropped it and it was an accident. You threw eggs at him on purpose. It's not fair.' Crasher jumped on to his inflatable crocodile and went chasing after Constable Dunstable, crashing into everything on the way.

Nobody would listen to Poppy or Crasher. They were too upset because there was water all over their carpets and their furniture was floating away

down the streets. Some of them pulled on
great rubbery boots and went wading
after the giant. Some of them climbed
into rowing boats and went splashing
after him.

Giant Jim looked out from his giant
bath (which didn't have much water left
in it) and saw the enormous crowd of
townspeople coming after him. They
were waving their fists and shouting

angry words. Some of them were carrying big pieces of wood.

Giant Jim was much, much bigger than any of them, but he was very scared.

'I don't think I like it here any more,' he muttered.

'Don't go!' cried Poppy. 'It's just that they haven't got used to you yet.'

'We all like you!' yelled Crasher, as his crocodile crashed into a tree and got stuck among the branches.

But Giant Jim put Florence Fluffybum back in her basket and strapped his saxophone to his back.

'I thought it would be nice here,' he told Poppy and Crasher. 'I thought I could be helpful and have lots of friends and people to talk to. But I'm too big and clumsy.' He got to his feet and strode away over the far hills and quickly disappeared.

'Hurrah!' shouted the townspeople. 'That got rid of him.'

'It's not fair,' murmured Poppy sadly.

'No, it isn't,' agreed Crasher, and he climbed off his crocodile, fell from the tree and crashed into the flood.

'You silly, clumsy boy!' laughed Mrs Crasher, and she waded into the flood water, rescued her son and gave him a big hug. Crasher turned to her.

'How come when I'm silly you laugh
and give me a hug, but when Giant Jim
is silly you all throw eggs at him and
chase him away?'

Mrs Crasher looked rather surprised.
'I don't really know,' she admitted. 'I
have never thought about it, but I can
tell you one thing. That giant is much
too big to hug.'

5 Help!

Once Giant Jim had gone, things quickly
went back to normal in the town. The
flood waters went down. The houses
dried out. All the animals went back to
the right fields. The library was cleaned.

'What a nice town this is,' said Mrs
Careless, the Mayoress.

'It's clean,' smiled Mr Sniffling.

'It's a peaceful town,' nodded
Constable Dunstable with great
satisfaction.

'That's because it doesn't have a
giant,' said Mrs Goodbody cheerfully.

'It's boring,' muttered little Poppy
Palmer. 'It was much more fun when
Giant Jim was here.'

'Thank goodness he isn't coming

back,' cried Mrs Sniffling. 'We are well rid of him. He was hopeless.' And all the townspeople felt very pleased with themselves because they had got rid of Giant Jim.

But the very next day the hurricane came. It started a long way off. The wind whistled round and round. First of all it spun slowly, picking up dust and specks of dirt and swirling them round. Then it spun faster and grew bigger. It plucked stones and clods of earth from the ground, and whisked them round like beans in a coffee grinder.

The hurricane grew bigger,
and stronger,
and taller,
and wider,
and faster.

Now it was so strong it could pick up dog kennels, and cars, and people on bicycles. It began to twist and turn and snake its way across the countryside, and all the time it was getting stronger and heading straight for the little town.

All at once Farmer Palmer saw half his cows go whizzing up in the air. Round and round they went, like fat brown balloons on legs.

'Help!' yelled Farmer Palmer. 'My cows are flying away! This is even worse than Giant Jim! Everybody hide – the hurricane is here!'

It was truly terrifying. Up in the air
went Farmer Palmer's sheep, a great big
fluffy cloud of them, bleating and
baaing. Then the hurricane hit the town.
Buildings were plucked from the ground
and went swirling round, high in the air.
Some still had people inside.

'Help!' screamed Mr Sniffling, who
was sitting on the toilet when all at once
the whole thing took off like a rocket.
'Put me down! I don't like this. Stop –
I'm getting giddy!'

But the hurricane didn't stop. It
whizzed faster and faster. One by one it

wrenched buildings from the streets of the town and whisked them into the air. Most of the townspeople were running away as fast as they could.

'Save us! Somebody save us!' they screamed as the hurricane came after them, but there was no escape from the great, roaring monster wind.

And then Giant Jim came striding back over the hills from far away. He stopped at the edge of the town and opened his wicker basket. Out jumped Florence Fluffybum. She closed her sparkly eyes against the bitter wind, plonked herself down in front of the hurricane, and dug her strong, sharp claws into the earth so that she could not be blown away.

'You must all hide under Florrie,' shouted Giant Jim. 'You will be safe among her feathers.'

The townspeople pushed and shoved and squeezed and squoozed until they were deeply buried beneath Florence. It was warm and dark and soft.

'It's like being right inside a great big duvet,' whispered Poppy in the darkness.

They couldn't even hear the great hurricane outside, roaring across the countryside, and battering Giant Jim

and Florrie until they felt as if they were locked inside a giant concrete mixer.

The wind whirled round and round Giant Jim. It whistled in his ears. It twisted his hair. It roared right up one giant nostril and then back down the other.

'You can't hurt me!' bellowed Giant Jim. 'I'm a giant and hurricanes are nothing to me!'

It was true too. The hurricane could not hurt him. It went roaring over the hills, away from the little town, and slowly it grew weaker and weaker and weaker, until at last it could not even lift up a ladybird it was so spent.

The townspeople came hurrying out from beneath Florence Fluffybum. 'You saved our lives!' they cried. 'Thank you!' Then they saw their town. At least they

didn't see their town. It had gone. The
hurricane had picked up all the buildings
and whizzed them round and jumbled
them up and set them down anywhere it
felt like.

Some houses were the right way up,
and some houses were on their sides,
and some houses were upside down,
and some houses were piled on top
of each other.

'Oh dear,' sighed Mrs Careless, the Mayoress. 'Now what are we going to do?'

Giant Jim grinned. 'Easy-peasy,' he said. 'I can soon put things right.'

'Be careful,' warned Poppy. 'Don't hold the houses too tightly or you will crush them, just like our Dance Hall.'

With immense care, Giant Jim picked up the houses one by one. Constable Dunstable stood on Giant Jim's shoulder and told him where each house went.

After an hour's hot work the town was almost back to normal. There was only one building left over. It was a great big, empty barn and it stood on top of the hill right next to the little lake. (It was only a little lake now because of Giant Jim's bath.)

'That's not mine,' said Constable Dunstable.

'It's not ours,' said Mr and Mrs Sniffling.

'And it's certainly not one of my barns,' said Farmer Palmer. 'So whose is it?'

'It's a building from nowhere,' murmured Mrs Goodbody.

'It's a Giant House!' shouted Poppy.
'Look – it is just the right size for Giant Jim.'

And it was too. Giant Jim lay down inside and the barn roof covered him over like a great big metal eiderdown. He grinned back at everyone.

'This is a Giant House,' he chuckled. 'My house!' Then Giant Jim grinned even more. 'I have an idea. Why don't you all come to my house, and we shall have the Grand Disco Dance here, and it can be a house-warming party too?'

Constable Dunstable frowned. 'It is

kind of you to invite us to your house, but I think you are forgetting something. We can't have any music because you squashed all the band's instruments and now they can't play anything.'

'Then I shall play my saxophone,' said Giant Jim, and he did, and everyone fell over. Then they picked themselves up and began to dance round and round and round.

'You are a very kind giant!' cried Mr Sniffling, waltzing past with Mrs Sniffling on his arm.

'And you are not stupid at all,' smiled
Mrs Careless, the Mayoress, graciously,
as she was twirled by Constable
Dunstable. 'You're just a bit big, but we
are getting used to that now.'

Crasher's Mum sneaked up to Giant
Jim, shyly put her arms round one ankle,
and gave him a big hug.

Giant Jim played faster and faster, until they were all whirling round like a human hurricane, and Crasher crashed into so many things he felt like a dodgem car.

Even Florence Fluffybum joined in and, as the sun began to set, the giant hen could be seen silhouetted against the skyline, picking up her knobbly brown legs and dancing delicately across the hilltops.

At last, when they were so tired that they could not dance another step, the townspeople made a big bonfire with all the rubbish left over from the hurricane. Giant Jim got out his giant saucepan and cooked scrambled egg for everybody. Then they all got up and started dancing all over again, and that night nobody went home to bed at all, because they were so exhausted that they fell asleep on the hillside – all except for Giant Jim.

He crawled into his Giant House and soon the metal roof was rattling away in time to his giant snores.